The

Wish

I Wished Last Night

Endorsements

The Wish I Wished Last Night introduces a fresh voice in middle-grade fiction. Shelley Pierce unveils what goes on in the world of eleven-year-old Jase Freeman as he learns to cope with life without his dad, faces the school bully, and struggles to be the peacemaker. Your middle-school child will connect with Jase and look forward to the sequel.

—**Michelle Medlock Adams**, Award-Winning Author of Over 70 Books

Shelley Pierce, the author of *The Wish I Wished Last Night,* obviously knows, understands, and loves middle-school-age children. Parents and teachers alike will have no difficulty getting even the most reluctant readers to delve into this story because it deals with issues they and their friends often confront. As a retired teacher of thirty-seven years and most importantly, a grandmother, I recommend that caring adults also read this novel, for it can serve as a marvelous springboard for discussions on grief, bullying, and heroism. Definitely, a good read and time well-spent.

—**LaRue Speights**, Retired Educator

Mrs. Shelley should make copies of this book and send it around the world!

—**Layne Miller**, Age 10

Shelley has a writing style that pulls you in and holds you. *The Wish I Wished Last Night,* is a heartwarming story you will not soon forget.

—**Amazing Matt Fore**, Award-Winning Humorist, Speaker, Entertainer, and Author

Shelley Pierce's first middle-level speculative fiction shines like a star! You laugh, cry, question why, and look up with Jase as he struggles with life's twists and turns and what he never expected it to be. Only to be left with an understanding far greater than ourselves! Reading this book is sure to satisfy, and I can't wait to share it with my students! Shelley Pierce is a rising star in middle-level literature!

—**Amy Pfaff-Biebel**, Middle School Teacher

The

Wish

I Wished Last Night

Shelley Pierce

Elk Lake
PUBLISHING, INC.
PLYMOUTH, MASSACHUSETTS

Cover and Interior Design: Cheryl L. Childers
Editors: Cristel Phelps, Deb Haggerty
Published in Association with Hartline Literary Agency
Published By: Elk Lake Publishing, Inc., 35 Dogwood Dr., Plymouth, MA 02360

Library Cataloging Data
Names: Pierce, Shelley (Shelley Pierce)
The Wish I Wished Last Night/ Shelley Pierce
174 p. 23cm × 15cm (9in × 6 in.)
Description: Elk Lake Publishing, Inc. digital eBook edition | Elk Lake Publishing, Inc. POD paperback edition | Elk Lake Publishing, Inc. Trade paperback edition | Elk Lake Publishing, Inc. 2017.
Identifiers: ISBN-13: (e-bk) | (POD) | (Trade.)
Key Words: boys, bullying, single moms, father killed in action, inspirational, teachers, family
LCCN: 2017952981 Fiction

Dedication

To
Jesus, the Bright and Morning Star
&
Tommy, my true love and best friend.

Acknowledgments

Thank you, Cyle Young and Hartline Literary Agency, Deb Haggerty and Elk Lake Publishing Inc., and the talented editing of Cristel Phelps. Through you, God has given me the desires of my heart.

God has given me many friends who are cheerleaders for me. You know who you are and how much your friendship continues to mean to me. Admittedly, there were days I felt I should hang up the keyboard; your encouragement and prayers kept me typing.

A few friends are also talented editors. Thank you for your patience in not killing me over, my, commas.

Thank you, Towering Oaks Christian School. Your teachers and children connected with Jase! Sweet!

My Blue Ridge Mountains Christian Writers Conference family—I love you!

My momma, who requested each chapter as it was completed. She tells me I am wonderful and believed when I did not. Keep fighting the good fight, Momma.

I deeply appreciate my family—sisters, children, grandchildren. You are a part of this book and me. Can you find yourselves?

Thank you, Tommy. You keep my story going.

I am ever thankful to God, the Author and Finisher of my faith. He is the One True Star. He alone remains and brings us joy.

Chapter One:

He sat on a bench watching two young boys and their dad play football in Pickle Tree Park.

He sat.

And he watched.

And he felt a stirring in the pit of his stomach he tried to will away.

He knew better than to wish on stars or blow the seeds off dandelions. Certainly, the last four birthdays taught him wishes are for those who believe in fairytales.

The older of the two boys yelled, "Dogpile on Daddy!" A split second later all three were in the grass, the father facedown and the boys stacked on top of him.

And there was laughter.

Drawn into the scene, he smiled a spectator's smile.

He watched as the three stood up, dusted the grass from their clothing and walked to the sidewalk under the streetlamp that had just come on. The younger reached up and grabbed his dad's hand while the older boy tossed the football into the air.

"Let's do this again tomorrow," suggested the older.

"Oh, please, please, please can we? Please?" the younger pleaded.

The bench grew cold beneath him. He looked skyward. The rule was clear—at the sight of the first streetlamp's light, it was time to head home.

Barely eleven years old, Jase Freeman had lived near Pickle Tree Park most of his life. He had his own memories of laughter with his dad and the now absent sparkle in his mother's eyes. Standing to his feet, he zipped his jacket, flipped the hood up over his hair and shoved his hands in the front pocket.

Slight of frame but not of heart, he was determined to escape average. He remembered looking at the galaxy with his mom and wondering in awe at the lights above. She taught him to look for the laughter and search for the good.

Life had taken difficult turns. Now she needed him to help her find her way.

He headed toward home with a slight skip in his steps. There was no sadness tonight. Only determination. He smiled again as he thought of the boys and their dad.

He wondered what it would be like to play football in the park with his dad.

He wondered how it would feel to be a big brother.

And he wondered how long would it take to help his mom discover the star that would light her way.

Chapter Two:

Click. Click-click-click.

Uphill. Always uphill.

His lungs struggled to take in air. Thigh muscles on fire and calf muscles in knots, he willed his legs to keep moving.

An eerie haze greeted him as he reached the crest.

The sharp, demanding alarm sounded through the haze. Click! Click-click!

The heavy air had a sickening, sweet flavor. His legs quivered from the trek. He turned around to take in the view, expecting a fantastic sight.

Are you kidding me?

The vast, empty land was colorless. Dry. Fractured and desolate. A single drop of sweat rolled to the tip of his nose and fell to the cracked earth.

W- w-what? This isn't possible. I've hiked uphill but ... the ground is ... flat?

Jase stomped his foot against the crusty earth and sent a shower of thick white dust flying that slowly turned red as it settled. The dust coated his face, demanding to be swept away before it robbed him of his last breath. The dust tickled his nose as if it were alive. A sharp pain seared his chest.

The volume surged like a tsunami and the speed accelerated. Click! Click-click-click!

Jase grabbed his chest—"AAAAWWWK! Click-click-click! Jase thrashed his arms as he fought the pain.

He opened his eyes to find himself in bed.

Am I bleeding? Breathe! Breathe!

Everything had been a fantastic dream.

"Lecty!"

The startled giant eclectus parrot sat on his chest. Her bright red tail swept over his face, brushing his nose as it swayed. She turned around, sharp talon tips pricking through his T-shirt. Lecty dropped a chunk of dried pineapple on his face.

"What are you doing? Get back on your perch!"

She clicked her protest and hopped to her perch, which stood next to the window by the bed.

Do I need a Band-Aid or a tourniquet? Should I call 911?

He pulled the front of his T-shirt open, fully expecting a chest that looked like ground meat.

Whew! Not even a Band-Aid! Yes!

"Girl, you're lucky I'm not bleeding to death. We might be eating bird stew tonight!"

Click! Click-click!

Lecty enjoyed the morning sun and usually kept the noise down while Jase slept. She clicked by tapping her grey tongue against her curved beak. When her clicking got loud and fast, Jase knew Lecty was afraid or upset.

He sat on the edge of his bed and looked around as if to find evidence his dream was not a dream at all. He glanced at his desk and chair, the only furniture other than his bed in his small, light blue bedroom. It was just as he left it the night before with his cell phone charging at one corner, the desk lamp centered, a handful of comic books neatly stacked in front of the lamp and a picture of his dad in dress blues. His backpack sat in the chair. No red dust. No dry cracked earth.

Jase checked the clock that hung above his door and jumped up.

"Thanks, Lecty. If it weren't for you, I would have missed the bus! I guess I'll keep you around after all."

He changed clothes, grabbed his backpack and stopped by the mirror for a glance at his unruly black hair.

He sprinted into the kitchen and looked around for a quick bite to eat. *What a mess. Not even a clean glass. I'll have to take care of this when I get home from school.*

He found a slice of pizza from last night's supper in the fridge. Once folded in half, the cold slice was gone in three bites.

He locked the door and headed to the bus stop. The neighborhood gang had already gathered.

Haley stood off to the side. She hung her head and played in the dirt with her foot.

Steve tossed a football into the air. It twisted as it flew to the treetops. He spun and caught the ball behind his back. Classic Steve move.

Danny and Deirdre, twins from up the street, were going over questions for a science quiz. Jase wondered what it would be like to be a twin and have a friend around all the time.

"Sup, guys?" Jase shouted as he jogged up.

Deirdre frowned. "We're trying to study here. Keep your voice down!"

Danny nodded at Jase. "Hi. I hope you're ready for the science test. You know how Mrs. Zimmers is. She'll make the whole class pay if one person fails the quiz."

Jase rolled his eyes. The twins always had their noses in a book.

Steve punched Jase in the arm. "Hey, what do you get when you cross a cat with a canary? Shredded tweet!" Steve laughed at his own joke.

"You get a canary that always lands on its feet!" Jase was proud of his own quick wit. Danny and Deirdre stopped reviewing long enough to laugh.

Haley looked up and giggled at Jase's punchline. Knowing he had made her laugh made him feel accomplished.

The bus's engine roared as it rounded the corner, and everyone but Deirdre scrambled. She took her time as she carefully placed the study sheets back in a folder. Danny took the folder and tucked it in his backpack. They took their places in line right behind Steve.

Jase waited for Haley to step toward the bus. "Go ahead," he suggested. After she'd stepped through, he picked up his sneakered foot and placed it on the first step.

His legs ached as if he had run a marathon.

Chapter Three:

The first bell sounded as Jase and his friends got off the bus. They hurried to their lockers and went their separate ways. Jase dashed to homeroom, wincing as he slid into his seat. His thigh muscles tightened in protest.

Mr. Houston, a Crumberry Middle School teacher of the year, was waiting with a grin on his face. Jase was glad he got to see him every morning. He looked forward to seventh grade when Mr. Houston would teach him Government. Until then, he was glad to be able to begin each school day looking at his grin.

"It's Friday, it's Friday. The best day of the week!" Mr. Houston almost sang as he marked the day's attendance in the roll book. Jase was sure every kid at Crumberry Middle School liked him.

After standing for the pledge to the American flag and a moment of silence, the kids sat and listened while Principal Drew read the daily announcements over the PA system. Mr. Drew's voice droned on about club meetings, loitering in the hall and the first football game next week. He ended his morning announcements in his routine way—"It's never a crummy day at Crumberry Middle School! Get to class and make the day count!"

"It's up to you what kind of day you will have," declared Mr. Houston. "Go out there and make good choices, do your best work, and eat your veggies!"

Mr. Houston stood at the door waiting for Jase. "Jase, I need to speak with you. Will you come back by after lunch this afternoon?"

"Sure, Mr. Houston. I'll be here." *Oh, man. Great. I wonder what that is all about.*

Mrs. Zimmers stood in front of the class, holding her grade book. She looked over the top of her glasses. She was tall, thin, and wore her hair in a tight, old-school bun on the top of her head. She rarely smiled and always smelled like hand sanitizer. Her pursed lips sent the message she was not in the mood to hear any jokes today. She was seldom in the mood for jokes because "Science is no laughing matter." Jase had to use great self-control any time she made that statement. He wanted so badly to make a joke about science and "laughing matter." Mrs. Zimmers' upper lip was missing today. Jase decided to keep his one-liners to himself.

All the desks held a quiz sheet, face down, waiting for sweaty-palmed preteens to struggle, crash, and burn.

"The time is now eight forty-five. You have exactly twenty minutes to complete this quiz. Keep your eyes to yourself. Begin." Mrs. Zimmers was stoic. One hand placed firmly on her hip, she stood at solemn attention. Her gaze was so intent, she reminded Jase of a prison guard from the movies. She scanned the class as if a student might try to escape.

The sound of shuffling papers flitted through the air. Jase took a deep breath and forced himself to focus on atoms. There were twenty vocabulary words to match with their definitions and one bonus question. That meant less than one minute per word if he wanted time to try for bonus points. His momma had reminded him many times to "never skip over a bonus question Jasey, always try your best."

Jase was pleased. He sailed through the vocabulary words with eight minutes to spare. He hoped he would know the bonus question. The bonus wasn't something kids could study for because Mrs. Zimmers liked keeping everyone on their toes with random questions.

He read the bonus question and his mouth went dry. Glancing up, the clock that hung above the whiteboard taunted him, each tick of the second hand louder than the one before. Each tock reminded him to focus or run out of time. He shuddered under the cloak of this creepy mystery.

He read the question again.

Lactic acid is produced in your thigh muscles when glucose is broken down during prolonged strenuous muscular activity. What is the cause of muscle pain hours after exercise?

Chapter Four:

Whoa!

Jase wiped the sweat from his brow. He read the question a third time.

He wrote as quickly as he could. He explained muscles, converted energy, lactic acid build-up, and post-exercise inflammation.

The rest of science was filled with Mrs. Zimmers' lecture on the electron, proton, and neutron chart.

Jase's thoughts swirled around last night's dream, aching muscles, lactic acid, and inflammation.

At the sound of the bell, Jase grabbed his backpack and hurried to his shared locker.

Steve was already there. "How'd ya do on the quiz?"

"Probably aced it." *That bonus question sure freaked me out.*

"Wanna give me the bonus question so I can look it up before I head to science?"

"Yeah. Right. Whatever." Jase knew Steve wouldn't cheat if he had the chance to.

"I saw you and Houston talking after homeroom. What's up?"

"I'm not sure. He asked me to come by after lunch. Said he needs to talk with me about something. I don't know what I did."

"Dude, I'd hate to be you! Good luck. Check ya later!" Steve took off down the hall.

Jase grabbed his copy of *The Lord of the Rings* and tried to work as soon as he sat down in literature.

Tick-tock. Tick-tock.

Mr. Houston needs to talk to me. Why? Think. Think!

Tick-tock. Tick-tock.

Name the two characters in the following conversation:

"I wish it need not have happened in my time," said _____.

"So do I," said _____, "and so do all who live to see such times. But that is not for them to decide. All we have to decide is what to do with the time that is given us."

That's easy, Frodo and Gandalf.

Tick-tock, tick-tock.

Mom can't take another problem. Think. Think!

He ran his fingers through his thick hair, tugging on it before letting go.

Who said: "May it be a light to you in dark places, when all other lights go out."?

Galadriel.

Jase wondered what it would be like to have the light of a brilliant star forever close by. Sometimes the night grew very dark. Sometimes the day was dark as well.

Ms. Teal walked between the rows of desks. "Okay, guys and gals, we only have a few minutes before the lunch bell. Complete this seatwork assignment by Monday. We'll go over it together so you can be prepared for Tuesday's quiz."

With her calm voice and sweet smile, Ms. Teal was the youngest teacher at CMS. Crumberry Middle School was her first teaching assignment. On her desk sat a vase full of fresh flowers. This week's arrangement was made of miniature sunflowers with some added red and orange maple leaves. She reminded Jase of Miss Honey from the book and movie, *Matilda*.

The lunch bell called for growling stomachs to chow down. Jase wasn't hungry. Instead of eating, he made his way back to homeroom.

Chapter Five:

Deep breath. Deep breath.

The clock above the classroom windows showed 12:23 p.m., but the overcast sun sent an eerie, almost-evening message. The autumn breeze blew just enough to cause branches from a nearby tree to scrape the windowpane. The chill of the unknown settled on the back of Jase's neck.

Mr. Houston was grading papers at his desk. He glanced up at Jase.

"Have a seat." He placed his red pen behind his right ear.

Jase wiped the palms of his wet hands on his jeans as he sat down. He winced as his thighs protested.

"Are you okay, son?"

"Yes, sir. My legs are little bit sore, but I'm okay."

"Oh, yes, I've heard Coach K has really been pushing you kids to the outer limits. Let's get to the reason I asked you in today. I've tried calling your mom and haven't been able to get in touch with her. She really needs to set up her voicemail box. She must be very busy."

"Yeah ... uh ... yes, sir. She is."

Mr. Houston rubbed his chin. "Well, I'm going to need to speak with her soon. When is the best time to call her?"

"I don't know, maybe it would be best if I asked her to call you instead."

Jase held his breath. His mind raced as he spoke. He tried to figure out what had gone so terribly wrong that Mr. Houston would need to call his mom.

"Well, you'll have to tell her the good news."

"Uh, what? I mean. Sir?"

"I have good news for you."

"Good news? You mean I'm not in trouble?"

Mr. Houston raised one eyebrow. "Is there something you need to tell me?"

"Oh, no, sir! I didn't know what I did wrong. I've tried to figure it out all morning."

Mr. Houston laughed. "Well, you can settle down now, son. You have been chosen by the faculty to represent Crumberry Middle School at the Bully Free Zone Conference next month. You'll meet with other kids from our district. You'll need to come up with a slogan for the school system."

"Seriously? Cool!" His words escaped in a high-pitched squeal. He cleared his throat and tried for a manlier sound. "Why me?"

"The teachers have noticed how you treat your classmates. We've never seen or heard you pick on another kid. We have, however, seen you take a stand."

"I've never thought it was funny to make kids feel bad, especially for things they can't control."

"And that's why you have been chosen. We'll need your mom's permission for you to be able to go. It won't cost anything. The conference is during the school day. All your teachers agree that you are the man for the job. But if we can't talk with your mom, you won't be able to go."

"Okay, Mr. Houston, thanks a bunch! I will try to get her to call as soon as she has time."

"Sooner is better than later, Jase. We need to make arrangements right away."

The clouds slid away from the sun. The rays reflected off the orange, red, and yellow leaves from the tree. A cheerful glow filled the room.

"Thanks, Mr. Houston!"

As Jase walked into the hall, he was taller than he had been that morning.

Who would've thought I'd represent the school in anything other than being the little guy? Steve's not going to believe it!

Jase continued to struggle to focus the rest of the day, but now for good reason. He was proud of himself and excited about the conference.

Still, Mr. Houston's voice murmured in his head: *If we can't talk with your mom, you won't be able to go.*

Chapter Six:

Janice Freeman trudged down the hall, shielding her eyes from the sun's rays that beamed through the window in the family room. She shivered and tied the belt to her robe.

Thirty-one years old, with a slight frame, she appeared frail. Her natural brown hair perfectly matched her chocolate-colored eyes. She used to be pretty. Her hair had been silky, and she'd worn her smile like a dazzling piece of jewelry. That was so long ago.

Catching her reflection in the mirror at the end of the hall, she wondered at the woman with the empty brown pools where sparkling eyes should be. She touched her mouth with the tips of her fingers. It said so much without uttering a sound. Her lips, light grey and thin, draped desolately downward.

She shuffled into the family room, reached for the cord and closed the blinds. Shards of light lingered through the slats as though insisting, "No, don't hide us! Let us in! Let us brighten your day!" She pulled the curtains together to silence the sun's cheer.

Dragging to the couch, she laid down and curled into a tight ball. She locked her knees to her chest.

Tired. So very tired.

Closing her eyes, Jase's mom sighed. A teardrop fell to the couch beneath her head. As she drifted to sleep, she whispered, "I tried today, Jase. I tried."

Chapter Seven:

Jase found a seat in the middle of the bus and stared out the window. The forty-five-minute ride home was full of chattering kids, cool air rushing in through open windows and hills and curves lined by house after house after house.

He replayed the conversation with Mr. Houston. He smiled to himself, imagining the brilliant ideas he would bring to the conference. Surely, all the other kids would be amazed at his intelligence. Mr. Houston would even have to make another call to his mother. This time to brag about his brainpower!

The squeal of brakes startled Jase from his trance. He grabbed his backpack and got off the bus. Haley was ahead of him. The twins followed behind. Steve had stayed after school for football practice.

Deirdre and Danny spoke in stereo, "Did you pass the quiz?"

How do they do that?

Jase turned and waited for them to catch up. "Yeah, I'm pretty sure I did. You don't have to tell me about your grades. We all know you make it impossible to get much of a grading curve."

Deirdre frowned. "Hey! What's that supposed to mean?"

"He didn't mean anything by it. He knows how smart we are, that's all." Danny was a peacemaker.

"Yeah, like Danny said. I didn't mean anything by it." The breeze picked up and Jase zipped his hoodie.

"Well, okay, I guess." Deirdre pushed her glasses up on the bridge of her nose and gave Jase a half smile.

Jase turned to walk home. Haley was already halfway up her driveway. The front door opened and Snoodle, her little white yippy dog, came running out to greet her. Haley dropped her backpack and laughed as her dog jumped into her arms. Jase was glad to see her happy.

She's pretty when she smiles.

The small town of Crumberry was tucked neatly in a valley. Jase had learned in third grade about their little hometown's history. Crumberry went back to the end of the Civil War, when folks began to rebuild their lives and heal from the pain of all that was lost. Crumberry, West Virginia, lay just south of the Mason-Dixon Line. The people that settled there were a mixed breed. The folks were mixed because families from the north and the south had come together to found the town. Although they had many differences, the empty places in their hearts was what brought them together. They all understood the price of war.

Folklore said the name Crumberry came from combining the last names of two women who became the best of friends. Mrs. Crum's family traveled from the Confederate State of Tennessee, while Mrs. Berry's family tree reached back to the Union State of Indiana. Both women mourned the loss of sons in the war. The town's people hailed the unlikely friendship as the beginning of healing. In fact, the sign at the entrance to the town read: "Welcome to Crumberry, The Healing Place." So Jase thought the story must be true.

Every August, the townspeople attended the Blackberry Festival. There was a special baking competition in honor of the friendship of Mrs. Crum and Mrs. Berry. Ladies baked all kinds of yummy treats with blackberries being the main ingredient. The two friends were known for their many uses of the sweet, juicy fruit. The Blackberry Festival was the highlight of the Crumberry year. Well, the Blackberry Festival and the County Fair in June.

Jase enjoyed the festival and the fair, but his favorite time of year was now. Almost October, and the leaves were slightly turning orange, yellow, and red. The days were growing shorter and in a few weeks, temperatures would drop. The leaves would be painted in deep, brilliant colors. His mom said God flung the colors through the air after dipping the tip of His giant paintbrush into fluorescent yellows, reds, and oranges. The splats made amazing patterns.

Good-natured, friend-to-everyone Jase looked past the trees to his house. He gazed at the window with the closed shades.

He walked with his head held high.

He walked with purpose.

He walked like a man.

It's such a beautiful day.

I have good news!

And the shades are closed.

Chapter Eight:

Jase stood tall.

Blue sky above him.

Painted trees behind him.

The window that shut out the sun in front of him.

The colors on the trees cheered him on.

He stopped for a moment before opening the door. Taking a deep breath, he exhaled and carefully inserted his key in the deadbolt. He gripped the doorknob so as not to make a sound as he eased the door open and ever so cautiously pulled it closed.

He placed his backpack on the floor near the door and left his gym shoes next to the pack. He crept over to his mom. He watched as she slept. Her slow, steady breathing gave the appearance of peaceful rest and brought a sense of calm to Jase. Deep sleep was rare for her.

He pulled grandma's crocheted purple afghan from the back of the sofa and tucked it under her chin. *It's going to be okay, Momma. Everything will be okay.*

Seeing her sleeping made him think of what Galadriel said. *May it be a light to you in dark places, when all other lights go out.*

How he wished he could find a special star to light his mom's way.

His sock-covered feet carried him into the kitchen. He loaded the dishwasher and cleaned the stovetop with an antibacterial wipe. He dusted his mom's knick-knacks that sat on the windowsill above the sink. Two porcelain roses, each with a multi-colored butterfly perched on the shiny petals. He handled the delicate treasures with care. His mom had told him many times of how her dad brought them to her from the base he lived on in Japan.

He rummaged through the cabinets and came up with a bowl of cereal for supper. He poured milk into a bowl and added the cereal to the milk. His momma had taught him this trick when his dad was sleeping. There is no clink-clink-clink of cereal hitting the bottom of the bowl when it's cushioned by milk. His shoulders hung low as he sat in the kitchen, eating in silence.

Bam! Bam! Bam!

Jase dropped his spoon in the bowl and nearly fell out of his chair. He rushed to the kitchen door that led into the backyard. Pulling the curtain back, he spied Steve as he shot an imaginary basketball into a goal that wasn't there. He dashed to the door and swung it open.

"Steve! Man, I've told you a million times not to knock so hard." His urgent voice hushed. "You know my mom is trying to sleep."

"Oops, sorry. But I gotta know what Mr. H said. Will you ever be allowed outside again? How long are you grounded?"

"Don't act so happy. You're gonna be disappointed. I'm not in trouble at all."

The two shuffled down the hall to Jase's room.

"Hello! Hello!" Lecty was glad for some company.

"Hello! Hello!" Steve answered, and Lecty turned her head sideways.

Steve plopped down on the bed as Jase straddled the desk chair.

"So, spill it. What happened with Houston?"

"You're not gonna believe this, but I've been chosen to go to the Bully Free Zone Conference in November! Mr. Houston said the teachers voted and chose me to represent our school. Pretty awesome, huh?"

"Cool! That means you get to skip classes that day and probably not have all that homework. Maybe even eat something better than cafeteria food."

"And work with other kids to come up with a slogan for the school system."

"Congrats, Jase! It's not as exciting as if you were in trouble, but it'll do."

"Yeah, right. Thanks a lot!"

"You know I'm kiddin'. I better get home. Homework won't get done sittin' in my backpack. Hey, I bet Lecty could do yours!"

Lecty responded at the sound of her name, "Hello! Hello!"

"It's Friday, Steve. What's the rush? You've got all weekend."

"I don't wait 'til Sunday. I get it done so I can chill the rest of the weekend."

Jase walked with Steve through the kitchen and into the back yard.

"You busy tomorrow? Maybe we can shoot some hoops or something?" Jase wished his friend would hang around a little longer.

Steve glanced over his shoulder as he jogged toward the street, "Yeah, sounds good. Might have to bring my little brother, though. Text me!"

Jase remembered meeting Steve their first day of kindergarten. He was scared to death to go to school. As he walked into the room, his backpack was almost larger than he was and his lunchbox was heavy. When he tried to put his supplies in his cubby, this kid named Chase pushed him to the ground and said, "Move it, squirt." Embarrassment washed over him. He was afraid to get up. In stepped Steve, the biggest kid in kindergarten. That was the day he found his best friend.

Jase watched Steve leave and wondered what it would be like to play football. And have a little brother.

I'll try homework Steve-style. Maybe he's on to something.

He slipped back into the family room and grabbed his backpack.

He checked on his mom once again. He exhaled a silent sigh of relief to see her in a deep sleep. *Sweet dreams, Momma.*

Jase's sock-clad feet carried him back to his room. He'd read The *Lord of the Rings* three times last summer, so the worksheet was easy-peasy to complete. Science? Not so much. He studied for next week's science quiz anyhow.

"Lecty, did ya sleep all day?"

"Hello! Hello!"

"You really need to learn a new word!"

Lecty squawked for attention until Jase picked up the small ball and hoop. Weeks earlier, Jase had watched a YouTube video of parrots like Lecty who learned to play basketball. Lecty was catching on quickly. After an hour of repetitive play, Jase placed Lecty on her perch.

"Night, Lecty. Get some sleep. We'll play again tomorrow."

"Hello, hello!"

"And we are going to work on new words too!"

Jase peeked in on his mom. She was still asleep. *She'll probably sleep on the couch till morning.*

Jase yawned and got ready for bed. He stood at his window and looked out at all the stars.

Maybe it was time to try a wish on a star. What could it hurt?

Star light, star bright, first star I see tonight.

Jase stretched out on top of his covers, placed his hands behind his head and drifted off to sleep.

Chapter Nine:

The red earth swallowed his feet with each step he took. The air smelled of old sneakers and the school cafeteria.

Not another soul in sight. His eyes scanned his surroundings. North, south, east, west—he didn't see a creature of any kind. Everything looked the same, miles and miles of dry, red terrain. No trees. No sky. Only redness. The putrid air hung around him like three-day old fish in an open-air market. *What's causing this awful odor? It's attaching itself to the inside of my nostrils ... I think I will smell it forever.*

With no other option, Jase continued to walk.

The clay treadmill exhausted every ounce of his energy. Walking, sprinting, jogging, crawling, and going nowhere. Thirsty, tired, and red, he sat down. He rested his head on his bent knees. He closed his eyes, and the world began to spin. His stomach churned. Finding it impossible to control the vortex, Jase decided to roll with it. He relaxed his body and thought only of what his plan would be when the ride was over.

The air transformed from foul to pleasant and the spinning slowed to a stop. Jase was afraid to open his eyes. Panic rose from his boiling stomach into his dry mouth.

He summoned the courage to look at his surroundings. *Fog. Thick, can't-see-my-hand-in-front-of-my-face fog.* The pleasing air now came in breezes. Soon enough, his stomach stopped its flip-flopping, and Jase walked into the breeze. The gentle wind carried the fog upward until it disappeared. The ground in front of him changed as he walked, each step bringing new life around him. Blades of grass, winding vines, and a cobblestone path appeared as the earth turned its red face around to reveal multiple colors.

It's as if God dipped His paintbrush into every brilliant color and splashed the air with one flick of His wrist.

Jase picked up his pace as the path of colors came alive. Thousands of butterflies burst from the cobblestone, each a different array of purples, oranges, yellows, and pinks. Swirling around him, slowly at first, and then accelerating. The whirling mass whispered in soft and peculiar voices as they encompassed Jase in a throng of confusion. What began as beautiful quickly became frightening. Winding vines crept up his legs. Jase's heart pounded from his chest to his ears. The beat grew louder but did not drown out the taunt of reeling voices.

Jase collapsed as the vines wrapped around his legs. Whirling, twirling, purple nausea, orange heartbeats, trapped in a tunnel of colors and whispers. Were the butterflies whispering or was it the sound of millions of frenzied butterfly wings? The last thing he remembered hearing was *you cannot go forward until you go back. You cannot go forward until you go back.*

Chapter Ten:

Jase tried to stretch his bent legs and found he couldn't. He rolled to the side and THUD! He rolled right off his bed! The sheet was wound tightly around his legs, around and through and over and under.

Oh, man! Are you kidding me?

Jase kicked and scooted to free himself from the bedclothes that held him captive. Once free, he wadded up the green and blue striped sheet into a ball and tossed it on his bed.

That was one crazy dream!

"Hello, Lecty. Hope you didn't have any weird dreams."

"Hello! Hello!"

Jase tossed Lecty a chunk of dried mango and put fresh seeds in her bowl.

Warm, but not too heavy sweat pants and a clean T-shirt were perfect for a morning of basketball.

He unplugged his cell phone and stuck it in his pocket. He was only allowed to have the phone on weekends. His mom didn't want him getting into trouble at school. She always said, "A sixth grade boy doesn't need a cell phone at school. He needs to focus on the books."

As he stepped out into the hallway, he saw light coming from the family room. Jase cautiously walked towards what he hoped would be the sight of his mom relaxing in the recliner, reading the Saturday paper and maybe drinking tea.

Jase remembered what life was like before ... well, just before. He remembered hearing his mom humming in the kitchen as she cooked. She would sometimes sing while she worked in the flowerbeds in the backyard. Jase thought it looked more like play, because she seemed to have so much fun digging in the dirt. His favorite memory though, was the fun they used to have stargazing. Jase was five years old the first time she woke him from his sleep late in the night.

"Come on, Jasey, I've got something to show you!"

She had Grandma's purple afghan, and the two of them stepped into the backyard. The scent of the rose bushes hung on the heavy dew and enveloped the backyard. Jase took several minutes to wake up enough to ask his momma questions.

"Why are we out here, Momma? It's dark! I'm afraid the wolves will come and get us!" He stood close to her.

"Oh, hush, silly boy! There are no wolves in Crumberry. They are all up on the hilltops, watching the stars. Look up, Jasey, what do you see?"

Jase tilted his head back and saw the stars glistening like diamonds. Momma spread the afghan out on the damp grass. The two of them stretched out and watched the stars.

"See how they shimmer and shine? The stars are winking at us, Jase. That's why God flung them out there, so they could light our way."

Just as momma finished speaking a bright flash raced across the night sky.

"Momma, what was it? Did you see it? What was it?"

"I do believe it's God's flashlight!" Momma said with a wink.

Even at five years old, Jase knew this was a game momma was playing. She loved to play games and have grand adventures without ever leaving the yard.

That night so long ago was the first of too many to count. As Jase got older, the two would wait for the black sky to light up so they could sneak away and gaze at the grand display of radiance. Jase no longer feared the night. Momma had taught him the night held wonders.

A long time had passed since they had looked at the stars together. And weeks since Momma sat sipping tea, reading the paper.

The blinds were open. The Saturday morning sun was extra bright. Momma was standing near the window watching a squirrel jump from one tree to another. The sun bathed her face.

"Morning, Momma! Want some breakfast?" *I'm so glad you're awake! I have news. Great news!*

"Morning, Jasey. No, no thank you. I'm not hungry yet. You're dressed awfully early. Are you going somewhere?"

"I was going to text Steve. We might shoot some basketball later … if that's okay?"

She turned and looked at Jase. "Of course you can."

"Thanks! Hey, want me to get you some tea?"

"How'd you know I was thinking about tea? I can get it."

"No, let me! Orange pekoe or pomegranate and raspberry?"

"Mmmmm, I think it's an orange pekoe kind of morning. Thank you!"

She didn't know how he longed for a normal morning. He would travel to China for the perfect tea if that's what it took to make her smile.

She sat on the couch with the purple afghan draped over her slight lap.

"Here ya go. Um … uh … Mr. Houston needs you to call him when you can. The teachers picked me to go to the Bully Free Zone Conference, and he needs you to tell him I can go!"

"That's great, Jase," she said without a smile. "How much does it cost? You know we don't have—"

"Mr. Houston says it won't cost a thing. Can I go? Will you tell him I can go?"

"Yes, yes, I will call him Monday. I'm proud of you." She lifted the warm orange pekoe to her lips and paused to inhale the tangy aroma. Jase watched her as she sipped her tea. Her shoulders hung low.

I'm going to find that star for you, Momma. It will be a light to you in dark places, when all other lights go out.

Chapter Eleven:

Jase sent Steve a text and they agreed to meet at the ball court. He grabbed a banana and guzzled down a glass of milk.

The screen door bounced closed behind him as Jase left the house. The sun was hiding behind a cloud. Jase zipped up his hoodie hoping to keep the chill out until he and Steve warmed up with some basketball. Fall was an uncertain time of year in Crumberry. Sometimes the day would begin with pleasant temperatures in the 70s that turned to rain in the afternoon and snow by bedtime.

Jase cupped his hands and blew into them. He liked cold mornings when he could see his own breath and the trees rained leaves with each gust of wind. The breeze commanded the clouds to reveal the sun for a few moments of warmth. He shoved his hands into the pocket on the front of his hoodie and walked briskly towards the park.

A flash of color slipped over the sidewalk in front of him and quickly disappeared. Jase looked up at the sun as it slipped back behind a cloud.

Huh?

Out of the corner of his eye, he saw more color flit by. Or did it flutter? Jase stopped dead in his tracks and slowly turned his head.

Two butterflies. Both were a tied-dyed mix of purples, oranges, yellows, and pinks. Jase stood still and quietly stared at the insects as they hovered over the bushes that lined the sidewalk. He closed his eyes tightly and slowly opened them. The butterflies began their ascent, weaving in and out and around each other until they were gone from sight. The wind blew through him and sent an icy chill from the top of his head down to his toes.

Get a grip, Jase. *Get a grip.*

He jogged two blocks to the park. He picked up his pace as he neared the ball court. He spun around to make an imaginary three-point shot. He heard familiar voices behind him just as his feet hit the court.

Steve sprinted up with a basketball and little brother Caleb in tow. Steve brought the ball to chest level and passed it to Jase. Jase turned, paused briefly and shot the ball with precision. Swish!

"Nothin' but net!" shouted Steve. "How come you never tried out for the team?"

"Not bad for a short guy, huh?"

"Shorty's got game!"

Steve gave Jase a fist-bump of approval.

"I want a turn! Let me try!" Steve's brother Caleb was six years old. He treated Steve like a sports superstar.

"Here ya go, bud! Let's see what you can do!" said Steve as he tossed mini-Steve the ball.

Caleb ran in circles as he did his best to dribble and shoot. The three played several games of HORSE, making sure Caleb won once.

When Caleb decided to dig through the rocks that lined the ball court, the friends began to play one-on-one. Jase dribbled the ball up the center and paused to take a shot just as a purple, orange, yellow, and pink butterfly landed lightly on the rim above the net. He closed his eyes and shook his head like a wet dog shaking.

"You okay?" asked Steve.

"Yeah, uh, yeah." said Jase, glancing towards the net. *Can you see the butterfly or am I imagining things?*

Jase took the shot. The butterfly hovered above the net. The ball rolled around the rim in slow motion before dropping over the outside edge.

The butterfly disappeared. *Was it there to begin with or am I losing it?*

The breeze whipped past Jase, bringing a muffled whisper, "you can't go forward until you go back." Nausea swept over him, and the color drained from his face.

"You're not okay. What's goin' on?"

"I just need a break. I'm gonna go sit down for a sec."

"I'll come too. Here, Caleb, see how many shots you can make in a row. I'll be watching!" Steve bounced the ball into Caleb's hands.

The boys sat down under a tree near the court. Jase hung his head and rubbed his eyes.

"You're acting really weird man, what's up?"

"I just didn't sleep so great last night, that's all. I'm fine. Just give me a minute."

"Hey, did you ask your mom about that bullying thing?"

"Yeah, she said she'll call Mr. Houston on Monday."

"Do you think she'll remember?"

Jase pursed his lips, and he shot Steve a look.

"What?" Steve shrugged.

Jase chose not to answer.

Chapter Twelve:

She had combed her hair that morning and placed a shiny silver clip in the back, creating a wonky ponytail. A little bit of blush, some lip gloss and she was ready for work.

She kissed Jasey on the forehead before leaving the house. He was fast asleep but would wake up soon to get ready for school. *Such a good kid. I'm sure Mr. Houston will let Jasey know I called. My Jasey, he is a world changer.*

She had been employed at the Quick Stop Market since the year Jase entered kindergarten. She'd worked her way up from cashier to manager. She was still at work when Jase got off the bus on Mondays. Her shift was twelve hours on Mondays. Her boss made sure she was home by four every other day of the week.

She often thought about what it was like before Jasey started school, and his dad was home. Cooking was one way she said, "I love you." She enjoyed placing bread dough in a pan, releasing the cozy aroma of yeast. She loved when good smells filled the air. Often, she would add a pot of homemade vegetable soup on the stovetop, simmering with goodness. Justin, Jase's dad, would come in from work, put his lunchbox on the counter, tousle her hair and smile a wide-mouthed, tooth-filled smile. She still had mornings when she woke up expecting to hear him ask about breakfast, or "Where are my work boots?"

They had decided together it would be best for everyone if she went to work after Jase started school. "Jancey," he had said, "you'll sit around and pine for the boy all day. That ain't good. Get you a part time job. Meet people. Let Crumberry see what a fine catch I got!"

He was right and she knew it. Her momma had said she was the best toy Jase ever had. Her entire life was her family. Getting Justin's lunch ready and then spending the day with her preschool buddy was certainly her happy-place. She and Jase would spend the morning making roads through the carpet with Jasey's Hot Wheels. Sometimes, they would take a break long enough to read a few books. Whatever they did, it was always an adventure. "Jasey," she would say, "there's a smile around every corner, sometimes you just gotta look for it!"

Justin deployed not long after Jase entered kindergarten and soon turned their white-picket-fence world upside down.

As she drove toward the store, her mind took her back to the day she'd met Justin. He'd been wearing his uniform. She had always heard there was nothing more impressive than a Marine in his dress blues. What she had heard was correct! She dropped her purse on the sidewalk when she saw him. They both reached for it, and her hand brushed his. He picked the bag up and handed it to her with a mischievous grin on his face. He was so handsome, he took her breath away. They began dating soon afterwards. She loved him from the moment she saw him. He surprised her one starry evening in the park. He went down on one knee and opened a small box in front of her.

"Will you marry me?"

And even though she knew her Marine might someday be

ployed, she said, "Yes."

One year later, Jase was born.

H ███████ as it been, Justin? I miss you. Jase misses you …
███████ re easier than others.

skipped going to his locker and went straight to homeroom.

rnin', Mr. Houston."

y, Jase!"

m said she will call you today."

lled this morning and left a message saying you can go.
okay? I don't mean to be nosy, but her voice sounded …
didn't sound … she sounded tired. I hope she's not sick

o, she isn't sick. She has had a lot on her mind lately.
nyhow, I'm glad she called."

"Well, okay then. I hope she's doing okay. You better get busy
inking of ideas for the conference. Time flies, you know."

"Yes, sir! I'll get on it!"

The blaring of the bell was music to Jase's ears. He wasn't sure
ow he could respectfully end the conversation.

His feet hardly touched the floor as he headed down the hall to
e his good friend Mrs. Zimmers.

She remembered! She called and said I can go! Yup, she remembered!

He literally slid into science class. The waxed and polished school
ors welcomed his tread bare gym shoes.

Mrs. Zimmers looked up in disapproval of his entrance, her thin
s pressed together and both eyebrows bunched into one.

"Hello, Mrs. Zimmers. You know what? I tried to read a book
gravity this weekend, but it was just too easy to put down!"

Jase saw a slight twinkle in her eyes, and she almost smiled. "Mr.
eeman, please take your seat."

A grin on his face, he skidded to his seat. Haley was already seated in the desk next to him.

"Hi, Haley!"

"Hi." Her cheeks flushed pink.

"I'll make Mrs. Zimmers laugh before Chri

"Good luck with that."

"You'll see! Wait, scratch that. You'll hear!"

She shook her head in a sort of you-are-cr

I'll make you laugh too.

Mrs. Zimmers placed two sheets of paper on each de

first was Friday's quiz and the second was seatwork for the

walked toward her desk and spun around on one heel.

"Several of you performed poorly on the quiz. You

you are. Correct your mistakes before beginning today's

corrected, bring it to me for verification."

Olly raised his hand, "Will we get half credit for the

"No, Oliver, you will not. The corrections are to help

coming chapter test. When you prepare as you should, yo

earned enough points the first time."

He starred down at his quiz. Clearly, he had performed poorly

Jase liked Mondays. The seatwork was usually easy and gave

hint of what was coming the rest of the week.

Mrs. Zimmers instructed the class to pass Friday's homewo

assignment to their right. The last kid on the right walked arou

and placed their work on the desk farthest left. Together the cl

corrected the papers so everyone had accurate information to stu

for Tuesday's test.

Lunch couldn't come quickly enough. Kids piled into t

cafeteria and lined up like they hadn't eaten in weeks.

"I wonder what's for lunch—mystery meat or secret stew," Ja

mused to Steve.

"Doesn't matter to me, as long as I get some!"

Laughter erupted from farther down the line. There was a b

Jase didn't know, red-faced and sprawled out on the floor.

"Did we just have an earthquake?"

"No. Fatty, fat, fat just couldn't get in line fast enough!"

"Hey, hefty boy, next time slow down and maybe you can st

on your feet!"

More laughter.

The boy sat up but didn't look up. He didn't say a word.

The guys shouting at the kid on the floor were a part of a posse who got their kicks out of making fun of anyone in the wrong place at the wrong time.

Jase shot Steve a seething look.

"Let it go, Jase. They're just a bunch of jerks."

"You ought to use your size for something more than pounding guys on a football field."

Steve shook his head as Jase stepped out of line and walked over to the boy.

"Come on. Get in line with us."

"Hey, Squirt! What do you think you're doing? No cutting in line! Pudge was behind us!"

"Well, looks like he's going to be in front of you now."

As Jase and the boy turned to walk away, one of the jerks shoved Jase in the back. Jase kept walking.

"Better watch your back pipsqueak. You'll get yours!"

Jase took his place in line and put the new kid in between Steve and himself.

"Thanks." The kid stared at the floor.

"No worries. I'm Jase. This is Steve."

"Hey. Brendan. Thanks again."

The rest of the lunch hour was uneventful. Uneventful unless you count the cold stares from one table to the next. Steve, Jase, and the new kid ate and talked football while the posse flicked food at each other. Jeff, the head-bully, just glared at Jase.

"Jeff is the biggest jerk in the school. Don't let him catch you off guard." Steve was trying to "big-brother" Jase again.

"I'm not worried."

Chapter Thirteen:

Mr. Tims was seated in his wheelchair at his desk. If he could have stood up, he would be a tall man. His broad shoulders and large biceps screamed self-discipline and upper body strength. Mr. Tims had served in the United States Marine Corps before he became a teacher. While serving in Operation Enduring Freedom in Afghanistan, the Humvee he was in rolled over an improvised explosive device. Mr. Tims was thrown free in the blast but his spinal column was severed when he landed. He didn't talk much about it, but when kids asked what happened he told how his Marine Corps brothers had carried him to safety. He did not talk about the fact that after taking on gunfire, one of the men shielded him from the bullets. Mr. Tims' life had been saved, but the hero who shielded him did not come home. Mr. Tims was a proud man. And he was a good teacher, even if it was algebra.

"Someone tell the class what went wrong this weekend."

Hands went up around the room. Mr. Tims called on Mandy. Mandy loved to talk, even when she didn't have anything to say.

"Well, my mom and dad and me ..."

"I. Mom, Dad, and I."

"My mom and dad and I went to visit my Aunt Kimi on Saturday and on our way home, we got a flat tire. Dad was mad and Mom was worried and I just read my book until Dad said to get out of the car. Mom and me ... Mom and I sat under a tree while Dad took the flat tire off and put the spare tire on. As soon as we got back in the car, it started to rain. Dad said, 'That was close!' And Mom said, 'I would not have been happy if the rain messed up my hair.' And then Dad said, 'You're beautiful even when your hair is a mess.' And then I said, 'That's disgusting'..."

Mr. Tims put his hand up and Mandy quit speaking. "Thank you, Mandy. Did you learn anything from that flat tire experience?"

"I learned it's good to always have a spare."

Kids laughed as Mr. Tims said, "Good answer. My dad always said, 'Expect the best but prepare for the worst.' So, there you go gang, flat tires in life are going to happen. Be sure you carry a spare."

Jase remembered Ms. Teal teaching idioms and was sure this saying about carrying a spare meant more than just a spare tire. Mr. Tims often taught the class to look for the good that comes out of difficult situations. He enjoyed throwing life lessons in with algebra. Maybe that's why Jase liked his class so much. Or perhaps because there was something about him that made Jase believe even a bad day held good things.

Mr. Tims instructed one of the kids to pass out Friday's corrected quiz. Many groans followed as scores were revealed.

"We will begin with the first equation. Jase, come to the board and write it out for us."

Great. *Wonder how many others missed the first one.*

Jase copied the equation from his quiz paper to the board. Mr. Tims asked Jase to step aside as he used his laser pointer to check each step.

"Take a look at step two. Jase, you miscalculated the sum in step two, therefore everything that followed was incorrect. You see, you can't move forward until you go back and correct the problem in step two."

"Huh? I mean ... sir?"

"You cannot correctly move forward to solve the equation until you go back."

"Yes, sir. I see now." Jase's knees weakened. He shivered as if an icy wind had blown through the classroom.

"Jase, are you okay?"

"Yes, sir. I'm fine."

"You better have a seat."

"Yes, sir."

Jase didn't remember walking from the board to his seat. The rest of the class was a blur of numbers and symbols and whispers, "you cannot go forward until you go back."

The bell rang and the class scrambled for the door. Jase just sat at his desk and stared at the board.

"A-hem."

"Oh, I'm sorry, Mr. Tims. I guess I'm just trying to figure everything out."

"The equation? Or do you have something else on your mind?"

"The equation ... and other stuff. Mr. Tims, how do you do it?"

"The equation or other stuff?"

Jase looked down at his desk and half-shrugged.

"I have faith, Jase. Faith, that no matter what happens or how difficult my day gets, God is taking care of me."

"That's hard to understand. Do you ever question your faith?"

"It's normal to question. It's important to find the correct answer when questions come. So, don't ever be afraid to ask."

"So, your faith helps you when you are having a bad day?"

"I put my faith in God, and He's where I get my strength. That's why I ask silly questions like 'what went wrong this weekend?' I know God uses the tough stuff to bring good in our lives. He also helps me look forward to being here to teach every day. My faith in God is important no matter what kind of day it is. He's not just for the bad days. I count it all joy!"

"But ... you're in a wheelchair ..."

"Yes, I am. And I am alive."

Chapter Fourteen:

No one sat with Jase on the bus, and he was glad. He had time to think about what Mr. Tims said. I count it all joy. That sounds like a riddle, but Mr. Tims wasn't joking around. His faith in God gives him joy.

Jase stopped at the mailbox before he unlocked the front door, tossed his backpack into the corner and kicked his shoes off on his way to the kitchen. He tossed the mail on the table before going to the fridge for a soda. He found a note taped to the refrigerator door:

Hey, Jasey! I hope you had a great school day. There are cookies in the cabinet. In case Mr. Houston didn't tell you, I called this morning and left a message. You have my permission to attend the conference. I'm proud of you! Love you, Mom

Jase grabbed a few cookies and an apple. He sifted through the mail. He found pizza coupons, credit card offers and an ad from some guy running for mayor wanting money and votes. At the bottom of the stack sat an envelope, hand-written, and addressed to his mom: Attention: Janice Freeman. No return address.

Jase placed the mail, envelope on top, on the table and went to his room.

"Lecty, ole girl, let's work on some new words."

"Hello! Hello!"

Jase held the apple up to Lecty. "Apple. Aaaaaaaple. A-PPle. AaaaaaPPle."

"Raaahhhhk! Hello!"

"Apple."

"Hello."

"Apple."

"Hello! Hello!"

Jase took his pocketknife from his desk drawer and cut a slice off the apple. Handing it to Lecty, he repeated the word again.

"Apple."

Lecty took the slice with her sharp talons, balanced on one foot, and nibbled the apple.

Jase tried again, "Apple."

He sighed and muttered, "Whatever."

"Whatever! Whatever!"

"No way! Lecty, you're smarter than I give you credit."

"Whatever."

Jase laughed and picked up his Lord of the Rings book. He stretched out and began to read. At least that was his intention.

Chapter Fifteen:

He kicked as hard as he could. The vines that were wrapped tightly around his legs shattered. Shards of splintered vines flew in all directions. He watched as the pieces floated upwards in a vortex until they disappeared. He sat up and looked around. A lone butterfly perched on his knee. The most beautiful butterfly he had ever seen. Huge with brilliant colors. Its eyes were blue, large, and bulging.

Jase peered at the butterfly.

Its mouth began to move.

Jase leaned in.

The butterfly puffed its cheeks.

Jase tilted his head and looked closer.

WAH-FOOF! The bug's mouth opened and a billowing cloud of thick and putrid multi-colored smoke erupted, cloaking them both. Jase gagged.

"I hate when that happens!" The deep, gravelly voice came from inside the haze.

Jase jumped to his feet and held up his fists. He turned in a tight circle, as he had seen prizefighters do before a boxing match. He searched the fog for movement, ready to defend himself against the voice. The haze melted away and his adrenaline surged through his veins.

"You can't go much further, Jase. You should go back now."

Once again, he searched for the source of the raspy voice.

"Ah-hem!"

Jase turned his head as the butterfly landed on his shoulder.

"Go back."

"AAAAAAHHHHHHHH!" He waved his arms wildly above his head and tried to run but face planted when he tripped over his own feet.

"What's your deal? I mean, come on. I'm a butterfly. I'm not a spider. I'm a butterfly!"

Jase slowly rolled over. He could feel his heartbeat in his cheek. He reached up and touched the road rash, pulling back right away from the burn his sweaty, salty hand caused. The butterfly hovered above him.

"Go back. You can't go forward until you go back."

"What, I mean who ... no, I mean what are you?"

"I'm a butterfly. Haven't you ever seen a butterfly?"

"Of course I have. It's just that I haven't talked to one. Ever. Or smelled one."

"Sorry 'bout that. It happens every time I eat the leaves of a crosshatch bush. I love 'em. But they don't like me, if you know what I mean."

Jase waved his hand in front of his face. "Yeah, I know what you mean."

"Time to fly. I've stayed too long. You, my friend, need to go back."

"Wait! Don't go! I have questions."

"I have no answers, just two words. Go back." And it flitted away.

Jase sat for a few minutes with his mouth open in disbelief. A talking butterfly. I've seen it all now. At least I hope I've seen it all.

"Go back! RAAAWWWK! Go back!"

Lecty's loud, obnoxious squawk startled Jase from his slumber. He shot out of bed and looked for the butterfly. He checked both shoulders. No butterfly. He looked out his bedroom window to the streetlight just coming on. No butterfly.

A dream. Just another dream.

He glanced at the clock, six forty-five. Mom would be home soon.

"Go back!"

He looked at Lecty, "I guess I need to talk in my sleep and say 'apple.' Then maybe you'd get it. AAAAAAApple."

"Go back!"

Jase went to the kitchen, opened and emptied a can of tomato soup into a pan. He fixed supper for his mom every Monday. She never asked him to cook. He wanted to help her. She worked hard and came home tired on Mondays.

He moved the mail to the counter and set the table.

He heard the front door just as he placed the grilled cheese sandwiches on a plate.

"Mmm, smells good. I might just eat two."

"It's grilled cheese Monday, you can have as many as you want."

"I'll stop at two. How was your day? Did you talk with Mr. Houston?"

"I did. Thank you for calling. I need to start writing down my ideas for the Bully Free Zone Conference."

"I'm proud of you, Jasey. I know it's not easy to be a kid in middle school."

"You can say it, mom. It's not easy being a short guy in middle school."

"That too. Maybe that's one reason you're such a good kid. You know what it's like to be picked on."

"I hate it. And I hate it when I see it happening. Jeff and his posse bullied a new kid today during lunch. I went and got him and told him he could eat with Steve and me. The posse got mad, but I didn't care."

Mom put her spoon down. "You better be careful with those boys. You don't need to get yourself in trouble. Stay away from them. What did Steve do?"

"He wanted me to leave it alone. I don't understand him sometimes. If I was as big as Steve ..."

"Jase, don't go there. You're not as big as Steve, and you can't try to guess what he is thinking."

They ate supper and talked about ideas, work, school, and Lecty. Jase told her about Lecty's new words—"whatever" and "go back." Mom laughed at the apple story. Hearing her laugh was better than hearing his favorite song on iTunes. Her laughter filled him with hope that one-day life would be the way it was before ... just before.

Jase cleaned up the kitchen while his mom rested her feet in the family room. She liked to watch Wheel of Fortune. She was pretty good at guessing the puzzle. He could hear her guesses he swept the floor.

"B."

"R."

"T."

"Back to the Future! It's Back to the Future!"

Jase dropped the broom and placed his head into his hands. He winced when he touched his cheek.

Back to the Future. Oh, my cheek hurts.

Chapter Sixteen:

Jase kissed his mom goodnight, washed up for bed and crawled under the covers. He gazed up at his ceiling. The glow-in-the-dark stars that hovered above him shown a pale kind of "I've-been-up-here-way-too-long" glow.

The crazy, bulging-eyed, talking butterfly with breath that smelled like road-kill told him to go back. Go back. Jase's brain couldn't slow down. After reviewing the dreams and events of recent days, Jase drifted off to sleep.

Where's that butterfly?

He didn't move all night. Not a single flash of color or flutter of wings disturbed his slumber. He opened his eyes to the sight of another school day ahead and no answers about going back.

The day was equally uneventful. Until the end of the day, that is.

Kids were scurrying to their lockers before heading to the bus. Jase turned the corner in the hall just in time to see a crowd gathering and hear laughter erupting. He pushed his way to the front of the crowd.

Brendan—on the floor, books and papers scattered all around him.

His eyes blinked back tears.

"Aw, Pudge is a baby. Go ahead! Cry, baby boy!"

Jase looked around at the kids who had encircled Brendan. Brendan sat up and began gathering his papers together. Jeff stepped up and put his foot down on a book as Brendan reached for it.

"I didn't know cows were so clumsy! Cry, pudgy baby. Maybe I'll let you have your book."

"Back off, Jeff. Go find somebody your own size." Jase leaned down to help Brendan.

"Yeah, somebody your own size." Steve stood a few feet away from Jeff.

The sound of whispers and mumbling came from the kids in the crowd as they all took a step back.

Brendan sat on the floor, red faced and disheveled.

Jeff stood firm, foot on a book and a scowl on his face.

Steve's jaw and fists were clenched.

Jase, stooping down to help Brendan, made a split-second decision. He reached for the book that held Jeff's foot and with one swift movement jerked it out from under the weight of the bully.

Jeff toppled to the floor in a most embarrassing sprawled-out mess of his own. Nervous laughter rose from the crowd.

The band of cronies rushed to Jeff's aid, but he shoved away their help as he stood and reached for Jase. Jase had turned to help Brendan up and was unaware of the looming threat that hovered over him. He glanced up as Steve's massive arm stretched above him, grabbing Jeff's wrist.

"You need to get to your locker so you don't miss your bus, Jeff." Steve's voice was steady and low, looking Jeff in the eyes as he spoke.

"Tell your pip-squeak friend to mind his own business. He could get hurt and we wouldn't want that to happen, would we?"

Steve gripped Jeff's wrist a bit tighter. Jeff winced. "No, Jeff, we really wouldn't want that to happen."

"Show's over, show's over. Everybody get on your way. You've got a bus to catch. Wherever you need to be, it isn't here."

Mr. Houston walked up and slapped the backs of Steve and Jeff. "What's the trouble here, gentlemen? Do we need to chat?"

"No, sir."

"No, sir."

"Boys, is everything okay?"

Jase and Brendan were standing up now, books in hand and ready to get to the bus.

"Y-y-yes, sir."

"Yes, Mr. Houston," Jase glanced up at Steve and over at Jeff. "We had a misunderstanding, but it's all good."

"I trust then," he paused and looked each boy in the eyes, "that we won't have any other encounters. Capiche?"

"Yes, sir." In unison.

Mr. Houston stood his ground while the boys went their separate ways. Steve and Jase walked one direction with Brendan in between them, and Jeff went the opposite way. A few members of the posse joined him.

Jeff looked over his shoulder and sent a cold, glassy stare Jase's way.

Chapter Seventeen:

Jase climbed on the bus, threw his backpack into a seat and slouched down next to it. He was sure everyone was looking at him. He was sure everyone knew. His scarlet cheeks and sweaty brow were like a giant, flashing-neon, tattletale arrow.

Way to go, Mr. Bully Free Zone.

Mr. Houston doesn't know what you did. Forget about it. Jeff deserved it.

Yeah, well you know what you did. Can you really represent your school now?

The guy is a jerk. He needed to learn how it feels.

Here's your motto for the school system—Bring the Bully Down.

"Hey, what was all the noise in the hall? What happened?" Haley asked.

Hot-cheeked, sweaty-haired, nauseating embarrassment.

"I just helped a kid out, that's all."

Haley gazed at Jase. "Well ... you okay?"

"Yeah, I'm good."

Jase closed his eyes. The sound of the rowdy bus crowd forced the voices in his head to pour out of the open windows and spill onto the street below.

The ride home was the longest ride ever. Jase jumped off the bus and began to jog. He tried to outrun his actions in the hall. He was certain his backpack was full of guilt because it got heavier with each step.

So, he ran harder.

Jase landed in his front yard. He dropped the backpack and laid face down in the grass. His chest heaved in and out as he fought to catch his breath.

He had tried to run away from what troubled him, but his mom was right. She used to say, "Jasey, no matter where you go, you take yourself along."

He rolled over and looked up at the clouds. They hung in weightless wonder like mountains of colorless cotton candy. He wondered what it would be like to float so high in the sky that troubles couldn't touch you.

God? I've made a big mess for myself. I never meant to make trouble. Please help me know what to do.

He was breathing normally now, so he stood up and dragged his backpack behind him as he walked toward the house.

"Jase! Wait!" Haley called. "You said you're okay. Are you sure? You aren't acting like yourself."

"Who am I acting like?"

"You know what I mean. What happened?"

Jase took a deep breath and considered telling Haley about Brendan, Jeff, the pile of books, and the bully that toppled to the floor. He decided not to.

"Seriously, Haley, don't worry about it. It's all good."

Haley's eyes misted and her shoulders slumped. She turned to walk away.

"Wait! Haley, I'm sorry. Everything is okay. Nothing big happened. Mr. Houston came before it got bad. I'm good. I promise."

"Some of the kids on the bus said it was Jeff. Did you get into it with Jeff?"

"Yeah, Jeff was there. But look at me, I'm fine! Don't worry about it, okay?"

"Just tryin' to be a friend, Jase. That's all. See ya later."

Haley walked away.

What a jerk. This day couldn't possibly get worse!

And then he noticed the blue Dodge Dart in his driveway.

That could only mean one thing.

Well, two. Aunt Christy was here.

And the day just got worse.

Chapter Eighteen:

Here we go.

He closed his eyes as if the action somehow made opening the door a stealth move. He pushed the door open.

There she stood.

With her back to the door.

Mom's sister, Aunt Christy, or Aunt Crispy as Jase had called her when he was little.

Aunt Christy heard the door and spun around.

"Jasey!" she screeched.

"Hey, Aunt Christy." Jase gave her a quick hug. "What are you doing here? Where's Mom?"

Aunt Christy poked Jase in the stomach. He hated when she did that.

"Aunt Crispy, to you! Ha, ha! What? What am I doing here? Why? Do you want me to leave? What do you mean 'what am I doing here?' Can't I come for a visit when I feel like it? Huh? Huh? Huh?"

Some adults are so obnoxious.

"Yeah, I meant ..."

"Okay, okay. I'm here 'cause your mom called me, Jase. She asked if I could come out for a few days. I'm just here to help."

"Where is she? Is she okay?"

"She's just really tired, that's all. She's in her room. I'm going to do some laundry, maybe put a few meals in the freezer and tidy up around here for a few days while your mom rests."

"I can do that, you know. I've been helping Mom a lot lately and I can handle things."

"Listen, you've done a great job, Jase. But you shouldn't have to do so much. You have a lot on you now that summer is over."

"I can handle it." He mumbled as he walked away.

The aroma of lasagna wafted past his nose as he traveled down the hall. *Well, her cooking will make having her here bearable.*

Aunt Christy was his mom's older sister. His mom described her as strong-willed. Jase always thought of her as bossy. She had a way of taking charge of everything. Jase didn't like that. He didn't like her annoying and ear-piercing laugh either. When she laughed, he pictured a pack of hyenas crowded at the edge of a cliff, all shrieking out over the abyss.

He had complained to Mom once about Aunt Christy.

"Now, Jacey," she responded. "You need to learn to accept people as they are. Show her some kindness, and you'll forget all about those things that irritate you. Besides, she loves us. That should be all you need to know."

Jase decided that he would not complain about her again.

A few days. That's what she had said. A few days. A few is three, right?

"Hello! Go back! Go back!"

"Hey, Lecty. Aunt Christy is here. You better not pick up any of her bad habits, you got that?"

"Hello! Hello!"

There was a sharp knuckle-rap at his door. Aunt Christy opened the door and peered in.

"Got a minute?"

Argh! No, please leave me alone.

"Yeah."

"I brought you something."

She handed Jase an envelope, yellowed from the passage of time.

"Um, thanks?"

"Just open it!" she said and she messed his hair up.

Jase opened the envelope with care and pulled out what appeared to be a hand-drawn map with crumbly edges.

"What is it?"

"This is a map your momma drew when she was about eight years old. It's the backyard we played in when we were kids."

Jase gently unfolded the paper and placed the map on his desk.

"Look, there's the swing our daddy put together for us, and there's the old tractor tire that was our sandbox."

Jase only knew Grampa through the stories his mom told. He'd died when she was just a kid. She had shown him pictures and told him how they would walk to a wild strawberry patch and eat until they had bellyaches. She said he would sing funny songs while he fixed things like her bicycle or the family's leaky bathtub faucet.

"This is cool, Aunt Christy. Did you show it to Mom?"

"No Jase, and I don't want you to show her either. Not yet."

"Why not? What's the big deal?"

"She made this map just a few weeks after our daddy passed away. She told me she had buried a special treasure, but she wouldn't tell me what it was. This map marks the spot where the treasure has been hidden all these years."

"Now that's really cool! When can I show her? I want her to tell me about it."

"You'll know when the time is right, Jase. I'm going to go put supper on the table and let your mom know it's time to eat. Wash up now, okay?"

"Yeah ... sure. Right away." Jase was mesmerized by the map. His eyes scanned the crude drawing past the swing set and the sand box. Past a ball and some trees.

And there it sat.

In the corner of the map.

A beautiful, multi-colored butterfly.
With bulging eyes.
Perched on the top of a tall blade of grass.

Chapter Nineteen:

Aunt Christy set the table for supper. She added the special touch of daisies she'd found along the side of the house. Yesterday's mail was tucked between the salt and pepper shakers.

The lasagna and garlic bread were amazing.

The supper time conversation was interesting.

Jase ate three helpings while he listened to the sisters go back and forth.

"And then she said …"

"Are you kidding me?"

"I'm tellin' you that is what she said!"

He wasn't sure who said what because his mind kept going back to the map and the butterfly.

"Isn't that right, Jasey?"

"Uh, yeah … I mean no … I mean, what?"

"I was telling Aunt Christy about the Bully Free Zone Conference."

"Oh! Yes, ma'am! It's gonna be awesome! It's next month."

"Jase was chosen out of everyone at school because the teachers noticed how he treats the other kids. Isn't that great?"

"Hey, you're lookin' at one proud aunt! Way to go, Jasey!" She reached over and messed up his hair.

ARGH! "It's really not as amazing as it sounds."

Jase replayed the hall incident in slow motion. The lasagna in his stomach turned to cement as Jeff fell to the floor.

"Son, you look a little green. Are you okay?"

"Yeah ... I mean no ... I mean I don't feel so good. I think I'll go get a shower."

Aunt Christy reached over and put her hand on his forehead. "You're clammy, Jase!"

"May I be excused?"

Mom nodded, "I'll check on you later."

Jase stood under the steaming hot shower until he ran out of hot water. He was hoping to wash away the guilty feeling, but it seemed as if it hung in the air attached to the steam.

As soon as he finished his shower, he looked at the map one more time.

Buried treasure, not long after Gramps died.

A bulging-eyed butterfly keeping watch.

He tenderly folded the map and slid the paper back into the envelope. He placed it in his desk drawer before he crawled into bed. He pulled the covers over his head, hoping to crowd out the voices ... *you're a fraud Jase. You're the bully who bullied the bully. Yeah, that makes it right. Jeff deserved it, right?*

"Hello! Hello!"

"Lecty, shut-up!"

He rolled to his side and forced himself to sleep.

Mom looked in on Jase. She uncovered his face and kissed his forehead, which was her tricky way to check to see if he had a fever. He was sleeping peacefully. She tucked his cover in around him and slipped out of the room.

She met up with Christy on the back porch and listened to the frogs sing their nighttime lullaby.

"How's the kid?"

"Sleeping. No fever. Must have just had a hard day."

"Good. He'll be even better in the morning after I fix him breakfast!"

"Thank you for coming. I feel better already! How long can you stay?"

"I took vacation days. I can stay all week if you need me."

"Thanks Chris, it means a lot to me."

"How long have you been low?"

"Seriously, Chris? Years, I think. Yeah, years."

"I'm sorry, I just meant that …"

"It's okay. No worries."

"Have you been to church lately? I think it would help."

"I'm sure it would, but I work almost every Sunday. We haven't been in months. I do the best I can."

Several moments of silence passed between them. Sisters can do that.

"Hey … do you remember the day Pop came home with that orphaned baby squirrel? Ma was so mad!"

Christy laughed. "Sparky, right? Boy, do I remember! That squirrel was so terrified it ran up and down every curtain in the house. Ma had a right to be mad!"

"Pop thought it was funny. Good thing Sparky was old enough to survive on his own. The marriage might have ended up in the same shape as the curtains. Listen, thanks for supper. You're still a great cook. I'll help you clean up before going to bed."

"Lil sis, clean up duty is mine. Go on to bed. I got this."

The sisters hugged, both feeling a kind of contentment that only sisters understand.

Chapter Twenty:

Jase opened his eyes and saw sky. Big, turquoise blue, sky. No clouds.

The grass on either side of his head was tall enough to tickle his face. He sat up and looked around. The grassy field that stretched before him held wild flowers, scattered in great clusters of red and orange, pink and yellow.

Eerie.

No breeze.

No butterflies.

No movement.

Anywhere.

So he sat, carefully examining his surroundings.

Which way is "back?"

As Jase scanned the wide-open meadow, his eye caught a glint of bright light nestled where the field touched the sky. Without thought, he jumped up and sprinted toward the light through red and orange, pink, and yellow wild flowers.

I wonder if this is how the Scarecrow felt when he, Tin Man, Lion, and Dorothy ran through the poppies.

As he ran, the color of his clothing transformed into a tie-dyed, swirling maze of red, orange, pink, and yellow as he passed through each cluster of wild beauty. The glint of light floated on air like a pixie fairy or an iridescent bubble from the solution his mom used to make for him out of liquid dish detergent.

Jase reached out to touch the light bubble as it danced in front of him. Just as his fingertips neared the bubble, it burst into multiple bubbles, each one its own shade of red, orange, pink, or yellow.

Jase froze in his tracks as the blue sky turned a sick shade of grey and the light bubbles became peering eyeballs floating all around him … dozens and dozens of eyes, surrounding him, staring at him. Filling him with dread.

He wanted to run but his feet wouldn't move.

So, he chose to stand firm and stare back at the eyes. He glared intently at the eye hovering directly in front of him. It burst and disappeared. Eye by eye by eye disintegrated as he set his gaze on each one.

As the final eye burst into extinction, Jase's clothes began to move … move as if they had come alive. Grabbing his shirt, Jase looked at the swirl of colors as they churned. He was amazed at the spinning hurricane of color.

The painted storm began to separate from his clothing, lifting Jase momentarily off the ground. Dropping him back on his feet, the mass turned one final circle and in a puff of red fog, swirled itself into the giant, multi-colored, bulgy-eyed butterfly.

"YOU! You faced your fear, eyeball to eyeball, and you won!"

"I … I … I did, didn't I? I'm glad you're here. Where do I go? Which way is back?"

"You must chooooooose to find your way, Jase. Choose or looooooooose. Soon, you will find your way! You'll find your way!"

"You're way late, Jase! Get up! The bus will be here in two minutes!"

Aunt Christy was standing in Jase's room with a blueberry muffin in one hand and his backpack in the other.

"Get up! Comb your teeth, brush your hair! Wait! No! Brush your teeth …"

"I know, I know!"

Jase got dressed in record time. Danny was climbing on the bus as Jase sprinted up behind him.

The bus driver frowned.

Jase grinned. His heart beating out of his chest, he found a seat and wiped the sweat from his brow.

The lockers were always crowded before the first bell of the day. Jase was one of the throng of students trying to exchange books. He opened his locker and a small piece of paper fell to the floor—one folded into a tight triangle, the kind of paper triangle he and Steve had used to play desktop football.

Steve reached over Jase's head for the books he needed.

"This yours?" Jase handed him the paper football.

"Nope, not mine."

"Are you sure? It fell out of our locker."

Steve examined it and tossed it back to Jase.

"Nope, not mine. Look, there's an eye drawn on one side."

Jase stared at the eye and swallowed his rising alarm. As he walked toward homeroom, the blueberry muffin rolled inside his guts like a loose bowling ball.

Shelley Pierce

Chapter Twenty-One:

Mr. Houston was waiting at the door.

"Jase, we need to talk."

"Uh … yes, sir." Jase dropped his head and watched his worn-out sneakers take him to his seat. The back of his neck was hot with guilt.

Principal Drew finished morning announcements in record time.

Mr. Houston's hands were on his hips. "You may talk quietly among yourselves until the bell rings. Jase, may I see you in the hall please?"

The hall was deathly quiet. No stragglers to break the heavy atmosphere.

"Mr. Houston, I'm sorry. I really am. I don't know what I was thinking. I'm tired of the way Jeff treats the new kid. I just wanted to …"

"To what, Jase? Fix it? Change Jeff? Make life easier for Brendan? Did you accomplish any of those things?"

"No, sir. I don't suppose I did. How … how did you know?"

Mr. Houston ignored the question, "Are you still the man for the Bully Free Zone Conference? Or have you become a bully?"

"No, sir! I mean yes, sir. I am still the man. And no, sir, I am not a bully. At least, I don't want to be."

"Here's how I see it, Jase. What you did yesterday to Jeff was no different than what Jeff has been doing to Brendan. Your life just got a little more complicated. I hear things and I've heard Jeff is not going to take what you did without revenge."

"I figured."

"You figured? Is that all you have to say for yourself?"

"I'm sorry, sir."

"Do you really believe you still qualify for the conference?"

"Yes, yes I do. I haven't been able to stop thinking about what I did yesterday. Even knowing Jeff is mean and probably deserved it, I wish I hadn't done it. Not because he's out to get me, because it's just wrong."

"You'll have to figure out how to make things right. It better not end in a fight with Jeff. I will not take the conference from you right now, but you are on notice. If you pull another stunt like this, for whatever reason, it's over. Capiche?"

"Yes, sir. I understand."

The bell rang and kids piled into the hall from every direction. Jase was glad that conversation was over. He was glad Mr. Houston gave him another chance.

Science class was on the edge of boring. Mrs. Zimmers' voice droned on and on. Jase's mind settled on the paper football burning in his pocket.

"Jase? I asked you a question. Do you have an answer?"

Jase opened his mouth and the bell rang. Saved by the bell!

"Complete the questions at the end of chapter seven."

Jase gathered his books and stepped towards the hall.

"I expect tomorrow you will leave every thought other than science at the door. Daydreaming is for little children and foolish adults. Do we understand each other?"

"Yes, ma'am."

Jase chastised himself on the way to literature. He knew Ms. Teal expected his full attention.

"The title of our series The Lord of the Rings refers to the Dark Lord Sauron. The Eye of Sauron was a symbol adopted by the Dark Lord. It was said that the eye saw everything and few could endure its terrible gaze."

Jase's eyes nearly popped out of his head as he listened to Ms. Teal.

Ms. Teal continued, "Frodo's description of the eye when he spotted it from the Mirror of Galadriel is printed on the whiteboard. Sketch the eye of Sauron and write a three-paragraph paper describing how you think you would respond if you faced the Eye of Sauron."

Jase forgot to breathe as he read the description on the board.

Floating.

Rimmed in fire.

Yellow like a cat's eye.

Terrible.

Jase's hands shook. His brain crisscrossed Frodo's description with the floating eyes in last night's dream with the eye on the paper football in his pocket.

Chapter Twenty-Two:

Jase caught up with Steve in the cafeteria. He plunked his tray down and immediately began playing with the mashed potatoes.

"Sup?" Steve's mouth was full. He never met a food he didn't like.

"Nothin'. I'm ready for this day to be over."

Maybe I should tell him. The butterfly. The floating eyes. Go back.

He glanced over as Steve shoveled another bite of potatoes mixed with corn into his mouth.

Maybe not.

"Whoa! Cool, Jase!" Steve almost bellowed.

"Huh?"

"Look at your potatoes!"

Jase looked down at his lunch tray. A mashed potato eye was staring back. He ran his spoon straight through the pupil. Without a word he stood, put the tray up, and left the cafeteria.

Steve shrugged and kept eating.

Jase took a deep breath as he walked toward his locker. As he neared the corner he heard voices. Muffled at first. Two ... no three—there were three guys talking. Near his locker.

Jase stood with his back against the wall and listened carefully.

"He's not going to get away with tripping me up."

"Good! What are ya gonna do?"

"Yeah, I want in."

"I'm gonna mess with his mind for a while. I'm gonna make sure he sees me watching him everywhere he goes. I'm just gonna stand back and look at him." Jeff's voice quivered with anger.

"Yeah, he'll get all nervous and wonder when you're gonna get him."

"I'm not gonna let some scrawny wanna-be make a fool of me."

Jeff and his posse walked around Crumberry Middle School like they owned it. Jase was tired of seeing them get away with hurting so many kids. Jeff's threats didn't scare him, not one bit.

Jeff is a lot like the Dark Lord Sauron. He thinks he sees everything that goes on at school, but I will show him. Good will win.

Even so, he decided he'd skip the locker and go straight to algebra.

Chapter Twenty-Three:

Aunt Christy and Janice had an early lunch and were out on the back porch once again, drinking coffee. Several mockingbirds nested in a nearby tree. The birds knew many songs. Janice could listen to them sing all afternoon.

"I bet you really enjoy your Wednesdays. Is it your only day off?"

"Yes, I usually do laundry all day and try to clean the house. It's not easy having one day off a week. It's a good thing Jase is a great kid. He is a big help around here."

"I can't believe how big he is. I really should come see you guys more often."

"So, how's Mom doing?"

Aunt Christy drank the last of her coffee, "Mom's doing great. Her garden is about done for the season, except for her pumpkins. You know how she loves those pumpkins. She misses you."

"I miss her too. Maybe Jase and I will get over for a visit soon."

"That would be great, it's not that far ya know. It would help you deal with …"

"Don't say it."

"I'm just tryin' to …"

"Well, don't."

That was the end of the morning back porch coffee break. The screen door bounced closed behind Janice. Aunt Christy decided to hang out on the porch a bit longer. She knew her sister needed to be alone.

Janice stood in the kitchen for a moment, scanning the room. The window above the sink was open halfway. The floral curtains, tied back by green braided fabric, gently moved as the afternoon breeze caused the curtains to sway in and out. Fall was in the air. Today's breeze was crisp and gave her energy.

She set her coffee cup on the table and noticed the mail, still standing between the salt and pepper shakers. She thumbed through the pizza coupons, Mr. Jasper running for mayor postcard, and an envelope with no return address. The handwriting looked vaguely familiar.

She pulled the letter from its safe resting place and began to read:

Janice,

I know it's been a long time.

You have been on my mind a lot lately. I just want you to know I am sorry for the harmful things I said to you after the funeral. I was wrong.

Please forgive me for the hurt I have caused you. When Justin died, his death brought back so many memories of losing your dad. I let my own loss, my own pain, cloud my mind. I know I can't take any of it back, but I'd like to start now and make a better future.

If you're willing, I'd love to visit you and Jase. I miss you.

I love you,
Mom

As Janice read the letter, the bitter tears that had been locked up inside her since her last conversation with her mom some four years before began to escape.

When Justin had died, her whole world had shattered. She'd tried to hold it together for Jase. Her mother's cruel words had pierced her heart. She was thankful Jase wasn't around when his Grandma Lynny unleashed her poison. It had not been easy to explain his grandmother's absence. Janice'd tried to satisfy his questions without revealing to Jase just how ugly his grandmother had been. It wasn't fair to be estranged from her mom right after losing her husband. It certainly wasn't fair for a boy who had lost his dad to also lose his grandmother.

She's sorry. After all this time, she is sorry.

She placed the letter back in its envelope and tucked it into her back pocket.

"Chris?" she raised her voice to be heard. "I'm going for a walk, okay?"

"Want me to go with you? A walk would do me good."

"Thanks, but I just need to clear my head. I'm okay, really I am. I just need to walk."

The front door opened and closed before Christy could respond.

Chapter Twenty-Four:

"I am Mrs. Ruppert. I am Mr. Tims' sub for the day. Do not ask me where he is or what is wrong. I do not know. If I did know, I would not tell you. It is not your business."

The class collectively stared at Mrs. Ruppert. She was short. She had big brown eyes and gold hair. Yes, gold. Her large lips were painted fire-engine red, and her eyebrows were penciled in place. Her perfume hung in the air, draping itself around each kid's face like a sickening old scarf.

"If you assume for one second that you will pull your middle school pranks on the sub, you are incorrect. I know algebra. I know middle school kids. I know what I am doing here. Open your books to chapter five and complete the odd numbers. Show all your work."

Hushed whispers moved over the room in a wave of frustration.

"Quiet! This assignment will be completed in silence! I am watching every move you make."

Jase watched Mrs. Ruppert's overly large earrings dangle as she spoke.

Everyone knew she was serious.

Everyone worked in silence.

Everyone, that is, except Mrs. Ruppert. She sat at Mr. Tims' desk and tapped her long, fire-engine red fingernails on the desk. Occasionally, she picked lunch out of her teeth with one of those fingernails, followed by a bit of sucking on her teeth and clicking her tongue against the roof of her mouth.

So gross.

This was basic review work from previous lessons. No new concepts or formulas. Easy-peasy. As distracting as tapping and clicking were, Jase finished the assignment.

Jase closed his textbook and placed his pencil on the desk. He glanced over at the clock, only fifteen minutes left in this class. Seeing the flicker of movement out of the corner of his eye, he looked at the long narrow window in the classroom door.

A pair of eyes stared back.

Angry eyes.

Burning eyes.

Glaring eyes.

The sight was a bit unnerving for a split second. Jase locked his eyes to the window like the red laser light Mr. Tims often used as a pointer. He did not flinch.

The angry eyes in the window closed and went away.

Jeff is not going to get to me. Especially now that I know his plan is to scare me before he pounds me. I will face my fear—eyeball to eyeball—and I will win.

Just before the bell sounded, Mrs. Ruppert stood and scanned the room. Her once large brown eyes narrowed into thin strips. Her bursting, bright red lips formed a "duck face" as if she was about to take a selfie.

Jase tried not to laugh. He knew the results wouldn't be pretty. Instead, his suppressed laughter came out in a horribly loud and too long snort.

The snort was all the class needed. Unstoppable laughter split open the room. Mrs. Ruppert's eyes became wild as she jerked her head back and forth trying to shoot a frightening stare at each kid's face.

The kids in the room grabbed their books at the sound of the bell and hit the door before she had a chance to stop anyone. Jase felt a twinge of guilt, but only a twinge.

I tried not to laugh. It was the duck face ... he laughed at the thought, no more snorting—he laughed. Out loud.

Phys Ed was the last class of the day. Jase looked forward to the current unit of Frisbee games. Coach Kirt reminded the class every day, "You are born with talent, but great skill can be developed." Jase was sure motto was Coach K's way of saying even if you stink at sports, you can teach yourself to improve.

Jase fell in step with the other kids who understood the drill. Stretches and warm up exercises always came before any physically active game. "Warm muscles are safe muscles" was posted above the locker room door.

At nearly seven feet tall, Coach K towered above even the tallest teacher. His head sat directly on his massive shoulders which had swallowed his neck. Everyone knew Coach K was clearly self-disciplined and lifted weights faithfully. Not surprisingly, middle school kids were quick to show respect and slow to disregard his instructions. As intimidating as his physical presence was, Coach K gave off the aura of kindness controlled by strength and strength controlled by discernment. If the world ever came crashing down around him, Jase knew he wanted to be near Coach K.

Coach blew his whistle in three short, loud, shrill chirps. Everyone stopped the warm-ups and gathered around.

"The art of Frisbee is fun if you know how to pull a disc and how to what?"

Mumbles made their way to audible answers, "Catch a disc."

"Brilliant, I tell ya, brilliant! And a disc is a what?"

"A Frisbee."

"I think you've got it! Line up! Two rows, let's go! Let's go!"

So began Coach K's disc drills. The first person in each line ran to the opposite end of the gym, turned and waited for the next in line to pull the disc. After catching the disc ... or running over and picking it up ... the receiver would then pull the disc and run back to the end of the line. This drill would continue until Coach blew the whistle.

Preoccupied by the duck face, Jase had forgotten one important fact of the day. He shared the PE hour with Jeff. Different teacher, same hour. Jeff's class was already outside warming up for an entire class period of walking, jogging, sprinting, or running the track. Ninety minutes of around and around and around. Jase would rather be outside than in the gym, but he was glad he had Frisbee instead of walking in endless circles.

Coach K had propped open the back doors to the gym. Every now and then a chilly fall breeze would blow through and give the clammy middle-school kids a reprieve from the heavy air that draped the insides of the 1950s Crumberry Middle School's gymnasium.

Jase kept his eyes on the door, expecting Jeff to slink into view. He watched the members of Jeff's class, clusters of kids traveling together around the track with apathetic hearts. Jeff and a few friends jogged, passing most of the others.

How long until he remembers I'm in here? How long until he makes his move?

Coach K's whistle interrupted his thoughts.

"Pair off, spread out, pull and receive!" He was a man of few words.

The rest of PE was more like a day in the park. "Pulling and receiving," was simply tossing the Frisbee back and forth.

Another whistle from Coach K, equipment returned to its proper place and one more school day was almost in the rearview mirror.

Jase skipped going to his locker and made his way to the bus. He saluted the bus driver, and plunked into a seat. Within minutes, the bus was full of kids past ready to go home. Jase slouched down, put his knees up on the seat in front of him and looked out the window. The bus pulled away from the curb.

There he was.

Jeff.

Standing alone.

Glaring at Jase.

Chapter Twenty-Five:

Jase laid his head back on the seat in the bus and fell asleep—a restless sleep full of floating eyes, Lord Sauron and an occasional duck face. Braided throughout the visions was a voice that whispered, "You're almost there! You're almost there!"

"Jase! Wake up!" Haley was shoving his shoulder as she spoke. "We're almost there!"

"Huh? Where's there?"

The bus slowed to a stop.

"Here's there. It's our stop."

"Oh … uh … okay, thanks. Yeah, thanks, Haley."

Haley grabbed his backpack and ordered him to get off the bus in front of her. He obeyed.

"What's going on with you, Jase?

He shrugged and quickly imagined what Haley might say if he told her about his dreams. Would she believe him if he told her they weren't just dreams? He imagined telling her about his mom … would she look at him with pity or just be his friend and listen?

Why are you even thinking about it? You know you're not going to say a word.

"Seriously, Jase. You never fall asleep on the bus. What's going on?"

She's pretty when she's asking nosy questions.

"I dunno, Haley. But when I figure it out, you'll be the first to hear. Thanks for waking me up, I'd hate to end up all the way over on Hackberry Road!"

"Huckleberry Road. It's Huckleberry."

"Yeah, yeah, Hackberry, Huckleberry ... whatever. Thanks for waking me up."

Haley frowned at him, reminding him of a look a teacher might give. "Go home, Jase."

She's pretty when she frowns.

Aunt Christy was placing hot cookies on the table when Jase walked in the front door.

"Hey, kid, how was your day?" She poked him in the stomach. Jase winced.

He grabbed a cookie, tossed it into the air and juggled. "H-h-h-h-h-hot!"

"Uh, yeah, they usually are when they have just come out of the oven."

He shoved the cookie into his mouth, gave her thumbs up and went to his room.

She followed him, "That might be all the info your mom wants, but that's not good enough for me. I want the scoop. The he-said, she-said. The whole ball of wax. The ..."

"Argh!"

She laughed and added, "Well, Jasey-poo? How was school?"

"I rode the bus, went to class, talked with a few friends, ate lunch, played Ultimate Frisbee, and got back on the bus. I had a day like any other day."

"You are a grouch. Better eat another cookie."

Jase was happy to comply with this request.

"Where's Mom?"

"She went for a walk after we had lunch. Said she needed some time alone."

"Aunt Christy! It's almost four o'clock! Why haven't you gone looking for her?"

He didn't wait for an answer. He grabbed another cookie and darted out the door.

Chapter Twenty-Six:

Jase went toward Pickle Tree Park. As the park was only five blocks from the house, he knew his mom enjoyed the walk and even more so, the duck pond. It was early fall, so the ducks had not yet migrated south. He hoped he would find her resting on a bench, watching the ducks do whatever it is ducks do.

God? If you can hear me, my mom needs the kind of strength you give Mr. Tims. Please help me know what to say to her.

He jogged, reconsidering the crazy dreams and butterfly sightings of the past few days. He was becoming convinced there was a reason for the dreams, and they weren't going away until he figured it out.

Go back.

You can't go forward until you go back.

You're almost there.

Floating eyes.

Facing fears.

Go back.

You're almost there.

He arrived at the park no closer to understanding. He stepped off the sidewalk and looked across the manicured park towards the pond. Pickle Tree Park was a happy place. Play areas were sprinkled here and there. Teeter-totters, swings that sang when metal chains rubbed metal hooks as they swayed back and forth, slides of every size, and monkey bars had been carefully placed by the town council. Clusters of trees offered shade for picnickers when the weather was pretty. The trees were half undressed today since the leaves had put on their fall colors, and several let go of the branches each time a breeze blew.

The pond was the centerpiece of the park. Benches lined the pond and were often filled with kids and their fishing poles. The pond was a catch and release place to spend a few hours on a lazy summers day. Jase had a memory or two of fishing with his dad. Mom would sit on a bench and act afraid of the bait, while Dad gave the instructions on how to properly place a worm on a hook. These were the memories that kept his mom coming back to the park almost every time she went for a walk.

On a day like today, most of the benches were empty. Jase stood by a tree for a few minutes, watching the breeze blow through his mom's hair. She sat looking out across the water. He silently slid in next to her.

She smiled at Jase, her tear-stained cheeks and sad eyes doing all they could to support the smile.

"Hey, Jasey."

"Hey, Momma. How long have you been out here?"

"Oh, I'm not sure, an hour or maybe three." She winked. "Jasey, do you remember the day you fell in the pond trying to reel in a fish? Do you remember how afraid you were at first? You thought you were drowning."

"I don't think I'll ever forget it!"

"Remember how your daddy scooped you up with one arm?"

"Yeah, that was the best part!"

She sighed, "I miss ..." Her voice caught with emotion.

Jase rested his head on her, "Me too, Momma, me too."

This was the most they had talked about his dad in a long time. After he died, they would talk about him often. Jase was glad for those talks. He didn't want to forget the sound of his dad's voice, the way his aftershave smelled or the thrill he felt when he heard the front door open and he knew his dad was home from work. When their days turned into this new normal, Mom's job and his school work edged out conversations. Jase thought about his dad every day but didn't bring him up. He knew his mom was sad and he did what he could to make her smile.

Jase's mother took a deep breath and held it for a moment. She slowly exhaled and put her arm around her son.

"Do you remember Grandma Lynny?"

"Of course. She's your momma. She has apple trees in her yard. Yeah, yeah, I remember."

"I got a letter from her. She wants to see us."

"Why?"

"Well, I guess after all this time, she misses us. She misses you."

"If she misses us, why didn't she write you sooner? Or call?"

"She tried Jase. After your dad died, Grandma Lynny had a real hard time. She didn't know what to do with her grief. You see, his death brought back a lot of sad memories for her. And sometimes, when people are sad, they say things they don't quite mean. I chose to keep you away from hearing things that might hurt you or confuse you. Sometimes adults make things harder than they need to be."

"That's stupid."

"No Jase, it's not stupid. It was all she knew to do. She was too wrapped up in her own hurt to be able to help us. But she is sorry now. She wants to be back in our lives."

"Are we going to see Grandma Lynny again?"

"That's why I've been sitting here by the pond this afternoon. It's hard for me, but I think maybe I need to go back ..."

A solitary tear escaped and lingered on her cheek.

"Momma? Maybe you should let her come to us."

Jase sat quietly and watched the ripples running across the pond each time the breeze blew. He thought about the apple trees and Grandma Lynny. He remembered apple cobbler and board games at her house.

Jase looked at the tear on her cheek, and he was sure he saw a rainbow glistening inside the drop. He felt like a little boy who needed his mom to tell him everything would be okay and yet, he knew he was fast becoming a young man who would protect her from hurting.

And he wished adults didn't make things harder than they needed to be.

Chapter Twenty-Seven:

Jase sat at his desk and worked on his homework. Lecty paced back and forth on his bed, occasionally uttering some nonsense.

He tapped the end of his pencil on the desk and thought about Jeff and his posse. He hated to admit it, but Jeff had unnerved him. How long will Jeff lurk around? Why is Jeff so mean? Will Jeff really hit me or just threaten to? And why did I pull the book out from under him?

Jase opened a notebook and began to jot down ideas for the Bully Free Conference. It would be here before he knew it.

Quiet the Bully in you: this is a Bully Free Zone.
Stop. Think. Change. I'm a bully free me!
Do the Right Thing! Build a Bully Free World!
Dare to Care! Bully Free Me!
Think Right, Do Right! Bully Free!
It's About Me. It's About You. It's About Time. Bully Free.

Jase decided to present his last idea. He also decided he would bring the others along to the conference just in case he needed them.

"Jasey-poo! Supper's ready!" Jase was sure Aunt Christy could be heard by the entire block.

"RAWK! Jasey-poo! Jasey-poo! RAWK!"

Jase smacked himself on the forehead in disbelief at what he heard Lecty repeat.

"Are you kiddin' me? Lecty! I told you not to pick up any bad habits."

"Jaaaaaaaaasey-pooooooooooo!"

I hope Steve never hears her say that. He'll never let me live it down.

Supper that night was hamburgers and homemade oven fries. Aunt Christy could be a pain in the neck, but everything she cooked made even her laughter easier to handle. Her hamburgers were the best.

"Here, Jase, this fell out of your backpack this afternoon." Aunt Christy tossed a folded-up, triangular piece of paper. "You been playin' desktop football when you're supposed to be studying?"

"No, somebody left this in my locker. Probably Jeff."

Mom wrinkled her forehead, "Jeff? Why do you think Jeff left it?"

"Who is Jeff?"

Jase showed the women the eye that had been drawn on the football.

"Okay, but why Jeff?"

"Who is Jeff?" Aunt Christy repeated.

"Well, he's sorta mad at me. Sorta, kinda watchin' me."

"Why? Is he still mad because you helped Brendan the other day?"

"Who is Brendan? Who is Jeff? Somebody pu-lease bring me into the loop here!"

Jase stared at the floor. His mother's frustration rested on his shoulders.

"Jeff is the school bully. Brendan is the new kid. And it appears Jase here thinks he is hall patrol. Answer me Jase, is Jeff still mad at you?"

"Uh ... yeah, but I ... well ..."

"Spill it, Jase. Did something else happen?"

The heat of guilt burned from the soles of his feet to the tip of the hairs on the top of his head. "Yesterday, after school, I saw Jeff and his gang making fun of Brendan. They had him on floor, calling him names …"

"Jase, you know you're not the bully police."

"I know, Mom. But there were no teachers around, so I went over and told them to knock it off."

Aunt Christy was puzzled. "I don't understand what the big deal is. Good job, kid!"

"Well, that's not all. I … sorta … kinda … well, I tripped Jeff. He was standing on a book and I …"

"Are you serious? Why? Why would you do that?"

Jase hated to disappoint his mom. "I don't know. I wasn't thinking. I just did it."

"Sounds to me like the kid needed a taste of his own medicine." Aunt Christy winked at Jase.

"No, Chris. That's not right, and Jase knows it. Does Mr. Houston know about this? I suppose you're disqualified from the conference."

"He knows. He gave me one more chance. If I mess up again, it's over. I'm sorry, Mom."

"You better watch yourself. Jeff will try to get you kicked out of school and the conference. You are not to fight with that boy, do you understand?

"Yes, ma'am."

"Aw, Jancey give the kid a break. He was stickin' up for the underdog."

"No. That's not how it's done, and he knows it."

The rest of the meal was eaten with few words spoken. Jase was relieved that his mom knew what happened. He was sorry he upset her, but glad the secret was out. He no longer felt guilty.

He had disappointed her. The burning on the soles of his feet hung around for the rest of the evening.

Chapter Twenty-Eight:

Jase shut his bedroom door and glanced over at the notebook on his desk. He hated feeling so conflicted.

Maybe I should just step down and give Mr. Houston time to find a replacement for the conference.

No, no, no! Mr. Houston is giving me one more chance. He believes in me.

Tripping Jeff was empowering. It felt good to watch him fall. That makes me a bully.

No, no, no! That makes me human.

I am capable of tripping Jeff; am I capable of hurting someone else?

Only if I am defending the underdog. Jeff shouldn't pick on Brendon.

Okay, great. Now I am justifying what I did. I am no different than Jeff. I am a bully.

Jase let out a heavy sigh and stretched out on his bed. Lecty hopped down off her perch and stepped up on Jase's stomach. She continued to hop until she landed on his nose. She turned her head sideways and said, "Jaaassssseeeyyyyy-poooo!"

Jase's eyes rolled upwards as he laughed at his feathered friend.

"Lecty, get off my face!" Jase sat her on the bed next to him.

He opened the notebook and began to make a few more notes.

He sketched out the words CHOOSE OR LOSE. Above the words, in a smaller script, he printed out choose friendship. Underneath the two words, he printed out Bully Free Me.

"What do ya think Lecty? Choose or Lose."

"Rawk!"

He held up the notebook and looked over the idea. He imagined all the posters that could spin off the CHOOSE OR LOSE theme.

"Choose to include. Choose equality. Choose peace. Choose kindness. Choose to think."

Choose to think. That one hit home. If only he had chosen to think first, he would not have tripped Jeff ... well, he would like to think he would have made a better decision.

"Rawk! Jaseeey poooooo!"

"Lecty, seriously, you gotta stop that before Steve comes over. Don't make me threaten to fry you up for supper!"

"RAWK! Chooooose peeeeeeace!"

Jase laughed and Lecty mocked him.

"Get back on your perch. Crazy bird!"

Feeling accomplished, Jase put the notebook in his backpack and washed up for bed.

She spoke in a hushed but anxious tone.

"Yes, sir ... this weekend ... I understand ... I'm sorry, sir, I realize it's short notice ... I realize I missed last Friday too ... no, I can't put this off ... I will make up the lost time, I'll work a double if you need me to ... thank you, sir ... I appreciate it very much."

She ended the call and put her cell phone in her back pocket. She didn't know Jase was listening.

Chapter Twenty-Nine:

Jase tossed and turned all night. When he did sleep, he experienced a whirl of Jeff tripping over and over again, floating eyes, and his mother's voice "I can't put this off." Occasionally, a butterfly would flutter by and whisper "choose or lose."

He was staring at his ceiling when Aunt Christy knocked on his door.

"Hey, boy." She opened the door. "Time to rise and ... you don't look so good. Are you feeling okay?"

"I'm okay, just didn't sleep much last night."

Aunt Christy kissed Jase's forehead. "Nope, no fever. Go wash your face, and I'll have some breakfast waiting on you."

He stood in front of the mirror and couldn't believe his own eyes. His hair stuck straight up like Lecty's feathers when she was upset. He had bags under his eyes that reminded him of the bulging-eyed butterfly. He decided a hot shower was the only cure for what he had.

The aroma of pancakes and bacon snuck under the door. He cut his shower short.

"Where's Mom?"

"She's still in bed. Seems I'm the only one who slept like a baby last night."

"A baby, huh? You mean every three hours you woke up and cried?" Jase had heard that joke from Mr. Houston.

"You're real funny, kid." Aunt Christy reached over and messed up his hair.

"Hey, watch it! I just got this mop to lie down!"

"Girls like the messy look."

"Ew."

I wonder if Haley likes the messy look.

Jase arrived at the bus stop just as the twins walked up. Steve didn't ride the bus on Thursdays. His mom took him early, so he could work out in the weight room before the first bell rang.

"I smell maple syrup." Deirdre wrinkled her nose.

"So do I." Danny eyed Jase.

"What? Why are you lookin' at me?"

"Oh, I don't know," added Haley. "Maybe because there's evidence on your shirt. Did you eat your pancakes or take a bath in them?"

Danny and Deirdre laughed in unison.

"Great." Jase looked down and saw the sticky shmear of syrup.

The bus arrived but if Jase thought that would save him from more smart remarks, he was wrong.

"Pancakes for breakfast?" inquired the driver as Jase got on the bus.

Jase darted into the restroom as soon as he got to school and tried to scrub the syrup off his shirt.

I don't know what's worse, the syrup or the giant wet spot in the center of my chest. Argh!

He grabbed his backpack and pulled the door open.

Jeff and his boys were on the other side.

Jeff grabbed Jase's shirt and pushed him back into the restroom. The henchmen stayed out in the hall.

"You're not such a tough guy when your buddy Steve isn't around."

Jase didn't say a word. His stomach rumbled.

"Well, what are ya gonna do, shorty? I could punch you in the gut right now and no one would know. No mark. No problem. What do you think of that?"

Jase's stomach began to roll, and the room began to spin. Lack of sleep? The pancakes? Fear?

"Jeff … you … should … let go … now," he managed to say.

"Or what pipsqueak? Let go or what?"

Jase had no control over what happened next. A mixed-up mess of bacon, pancakes, maple syrup, and milk came up and spewed all over Jeff.

Jeff screamed and let go of Jase just as round two slopped on Jeff's shoes.

Jeff gagged and his face began to resemble the colorless wonder of a field of snow.

Jase grabbed some paper towels and wiped his mouth.

"I told you to let go."

Jeff seethed as Jase walked out of the restroom.

"I wouldn't go in there," he said to the confused-looking bunch as he walked past them.

The last thing Jase heard was the sound of Jeff's gang heaving.

Later that morning, rumors began to circulate Jeff had gotten sick and gone home early. Jase didn't tell anyone about puking on Jeff. He was a little embarrassed but more relieved. Today would be a bully free day at Crumberry Middle School.

Chapter Thirty:

Steve barreled around the corner and nearly flattened Jase.

"Whoa, whoa! Where's the fire?"

"Jase! You're okay!"

"Yeah, but you almost took care of that. What's up?"

"Jill said Jeff and his posse followed you into the restroom. Are you sure you're okay?"

"I'm good. Jeff isn't so good. Jeff is, well, let's just say he's a mess."

Steve fist bumped Jase.

"Way to go buddy!"

"I didn't fight him. The situation sorta took care of itself."

"Okay, whatever. Glad you're okay ... uh, what's that smell?"

Mr. Houston stood at the front of the room as one by one the kids found their way to a desk.

"Tonight is the first football game for Crumberry Middle School. I hope to see each of you back tonight to cheer for the team."

The middle school played their games on Thursdays each week, leaving Friday nights free for Crumberry High's games. Jase had forgotten to ask his mom if he could go. She used to watch the pro games with his dad on Sunday afternoons. Jase couldn't remember her watching a single football game since his dad's funeral. Middle-school football wouldn't even be on her radar.

Maybe Aunt Christy will want to go. Oh, man! What am I thinking? Aunt Christy around my friends? What a disaster!

The bell gave the order to go to Mrs. Zimmers' class. The kids bunched up in groups of friends and excitedly talked about the game. Jase heard a few girls talking about coming to the game to watch Steve. He wondered what it was like to be a tall athlete.

Jase walked into science and noticed the room was set up for a movie. He groaned. These movies were made by the most boring people on earth.

"We are preparing today for the final exam on atoms. Please take notes during our film today titled Simple Science: Dissecting the Atom. Take thorough notes. You'll want to study them tonight in preparation for tomorrow's exam."

Murmurs began in the back of the room and like an angry ocean wave, crashed forward getting louder at they traveled.

Mrs. Zimmers stood straight with her shoulders back. Her face held the expression of utter disbelief over what she had just witnessed. She rapped a ruler on the edge of her desk.

"Excuse me!"

"Mrs. Zimmers, the first football game of the season is tonight and we—" Jase was either brave or stupid for speaking up, he wasn't sure which.

"EX-CUSE ME! I am not concerned with the folly of football! We will not discuss it further unless, of course, you would prefer to take your exam TODAY!"

The statement sucked the air out of the room. No one was prepared to take the exam today and everyone knew it.

Not another word was spoken.

Mrs. Zimmers pushed play and the narrator droned on.

Jase's eyelids drooped under the weight of the sleepless night combined with the remnant of high carb pancakes and the definition of electrons.

Chapter Thirty-One:

There is an art to sleeping while sitting up. Most middle school boys are born with the ability to remain undetected while sleeping through boring science movies.

The narrator began the introduction, "Our amazing world is made up of billions of ..."

The air was cold and the sky was bright. The ground beneath Jase's feet twinkled with shimmering lights as far as he could see. He stepped forward, walking on a carpet of glitter. The ground went up hill and the familiar burn in his legs simmered from the inside out.

A breeze moved past him in gentle, refreshing wisps. Was it whispering in his ear? Was it his imagination? He crested the hill to find a rocky terrain ahead. Rocks, boulders, pebbles, and stones scattered in pattern-less masses. The glitter-lights that once formed a bedazzled carpet now peeked randomly from behind the rocks. They were no longer white lights but were now lights of every hue on the color wheel.

Jase had no choice but to press onward.

Go back.

Almost there.

Go back.

You've almost found your way.

You can't go forward until you go back.

The breeze was no longer gentle. The air moved in giant colored swirls that reminded Jase of rainbow sherbet. He eyed a boulder that was nearly as tall as he and scrambled to stand on its pinnacle. The wind whipped against his clothing. For a moment, he thought he would topple down. He turned his face upwards. The colored clouds began to crowd the once bright sky. The clouds whirled and twirled in kaleidoscope fashion.

The colored lights that emanated from the rocks below blinked in a slow fade. Jase's heart skipped a beat. His eyes darted up towards the abstract art in the sky and back down to the laser show below. There was no sound, not even the sound of the wind. The silence was deafening. The flood of colors in the clouds and lights below made his head whirl. As the world blurred,

He lost his balance and took a nose-dive.

Just as Jase thought he would plummet to the rocks beneath him, the squall draped a blanket of calm gently around him. From chaos to peace in an instant. Jase sat down on the rock and breathed a great sigh of relief.

The silence was replaced by a distant thunder, a strange and scary rumble that resembled a fighter jet breaking the sound barrier. Jase squinted and searched for a source of the boom. Motion beneath him caught his eye. A tiny pebble on a small rock vibrated and began to bounce. The roar grew louder, forcing Jase to look up. The ground far beyond him swelled as if someone had taken his calm blanket and shook it in slow motion. There was no time to waste as the earth rolled forward, growing faster and louder. Soon, it would crest and send him flying.

In a panic, he searched for something, anything to anchor himself. His desperate fingers grasped at the boulder, exploring for any nook or cranny. The smooth surface laughed at him. The boom peaked beneath him and sent him airborne.

He tried to scream but no sound came. He soared upwards in weightless insecurity. It reminded him of that split second at the height of a roller coaster, just as the car began its descent and tossed him off his seat. He reached the height of his ascent and time stood still. He floated for several seconds before he plunged. His stomach fluttered and protested. His body rolled and forced his face downward to view the rocks far below. Again, he tried to scream but no sound came out.

Swoosh!

Swoosh!

Swoosh!

A streak of reds, blues, yellows, and greens swooshed in next to him.

"You can fly, Jase! You can fly! Stretch out your arms and believe!" The bulging eyed butterfly ordered.

Jase felt nothing but terror as he imagined himself broken on impact.

"Stretch, Jase! Stretch before you fall! You're almost FREEEEE!"

"MR. FREEMAN! Jase Freeman! Get down this instant!"

Laughter erupted. Jase became aware he stood perched on his desk, bottom pushed back, shoulders forward and arms outstretched … ready to take flight.

"Mr. Freeman! Take your seat!"

He slouched and crawled into his chair, wishing he could press himself into the seat and disappear.

The laughter almost drowned out the sound of the bell. Jase gathered his books and stood up.

"Mr. Freeman, you will stay after class."

"Yes, ma'am."

The kids clamored out of the room excited about the spectacle.

"Did you see him flap his arms?"

"That was hil-a-ri-ous!"

"I wish I had my phone ready."

"Guess what? I did! Look here …"

Oh, no ... within seconds the entire school is going to ... oh, no ...

The door closed, and Jase was surrounded by the vacuum of empty space and Mrs. Zimmers standing in front of him. She stared at him with arms crossed, lips pressed tightly together, eye-brows crunched in disapproval.

His head hung low. He had no words.

What happened next amazed him.

Chapter Thirty-Two:

"Sit back down, Mr. Freeman."

"Yes, ma'am."

Jase braced himself for the "I'm very disappointed in you" talk or perhaps there would be a long awkward silence. Either way, it wouldn't be good. It couldn't be good. Never in the history of Crumberry Middle School had Mrs. Zimmers been known to be a sweetheart of compassion and understanding.

Mrs. Zimmers pulled a chair over in front of Jase's desk, sat down and folded her hands.

And there it began … the long awkward silence.

Jase avoided eye contact while he waited for the crushing blow of discipline.

First, she cleared her throat. Then she spoke.

"I am only going to ask you one question, one time, Mr. Freeman. I expect you will be creative with your answer, but you best be honest with me. Your behavior has been erratic this week. Today … disruptive. Why?"

Jase took a deep breath and slowly exhaled.

"I'm sorry, Mrs. Zimmers. Really, I am. There's a lot going on at home. I haven't been sleeping well lately ... I just have a lot on my mind. It won't happen again. I promise. I'm sorry, I'm really sorry."

Summoning the courage, Jase raised his head and looked Mrs. Zimmers in the eyes. He was surprised at what he saw.

Kindness?

Pity?

Empathy?

Her eyebrows relaxed and her lips were no longer pursed. Her eyes had softened.

She cleared her throat once again.

"You have been a good student, Jase Freeman. I believe you are telling me the truth. Now, listen to me. I understand how difficult life can be when you are growing up with a single mom who struggles to make ends meet. I understand how easy it is to feel stress and at the same time, want to fix what's wrong."

She swallowed hard.

Are those tears in her eyes?

"Have you ever heard the saying 'hurting people hurt people'? It means that when a person is going through a difficult time and his heart aches, he might lash out and hurt other people. Let me remind you, you are not the only one at CMS dealing with difficulties in life. SOME kids without daddies grow up to be school teachers, hoping to make a difference for others. Some kids turn into bullies because picking on others is a distraction to the hurt inside somehow. Then there are kids like you. It is simply not fair that you must grow up without your dad, but you haven't allowed it to make you bitter. You continue to look for the good in other people and try to help the underdog."

Jase sat quietly trying to take it all in.

"We are all on a journey, Jase. Look around you. Realize the bullies in life need someone to understand them. Everyone has a story to tell. Not everyone is ready to tell it."

"I never thought of it that way before."

"There will be no discipline for what happened today. I believe the video that has probably already circulated is punishment enough. However, it will not happen again …"

"Oh, yes, Mrs. Zimmers, I mean no, Mrs. Zimmers. It will never happen again. Thank you."

Jase was halfway to the door when Mrs. Zimmers spoke again.

"Jase, you can't solve tomorrow's troubles with worry. Let tomorrow take care of itself. The birds don't worry about what they will eat and they are taken care of, you will be taken care of as well. Try to have faith that everything is going to be fine."

"I will try."

"Oh, and Jase?"

"Yes, ma'am?"

Her frown returned. "What's that smell?"

Chapter Thirty-Three:

He stepped into the hall and replayed the conversation in his head.

Did that really just happen? Kindness. Advice? A possible tear or two? Mrs. Zimmers has a heart!

Snickers and snorts and whispers interrupted Jase's thoughts. He didn't need to look around. He knew it was the video. Truth be known, if he were on the watching side instead of the starring-role side, he would laugh too.

So, he took a bow.

"Thank you, thank you, thank you! Autograph line forms to the right!"

Danny and Deirdre were waiting for him.

"You're just crazy," announced Deirdre.

"Certifiable." Danny agreed.

"Are you asking for my autograph?"

"Uh, no thanks." Two people, one answer, in one accord.

"If ya change your mind you know where to find me!" He called out as he walked away.

Will I survive this day? It isn't even lunchtime and I almost got beat up, I threw up all over the school bully, I smell like puke and maple syrup, I fell asleep in science class and I'm gonna be known all over school as the flying clown.

Jase was relieved when Ms. Teal let the class play classroom Jeopardy to review for the chapter test coming up on Monday. Ms. Teal was a Crumberry Middle School football fan. She never gave a big exam the morning after a football game. She was even wearing her Crumberry Wildcats T-shirt to show her school spirit.

Jase almost ran to his locker hoping to get his books put up before seeing Steve. He wasn't sure how he was going to explain himself to his friend. Shutting the locker, he turned to leave and bumped into Steve's chest.

Busted.

Steve just stood there and grinned.

"Oh, uh … hey. You ready for lunch?"

Steve's grin was causing Jase pain. His pride, well, what was left of his pride, was crushed.

"You're a legend. The talk of the school. I hear you can fly!"

"Yeah, well." He sighed. He had nothing to say.

Steve messed up his hair and opened the locker.

"You've got a lot of guts. I'll say that much for you."

Jase waited for Steve to finish at the locker. They made their way through the crowded hall to the cafeteria. Whispers and jeers and jokes rose above the throng of middle-school kids and hung in the air like a pirate's skull and cross bones flag.

"There he goes!"

"Is that him?"

"There goes bird-man!"

"Poor kid."

"Glad it's him and not me."

"Did you see the video? I've got it saved."

"I can fly! I can fly!"

Jase refused to look down. He smiled and nodded and forced himself to act amused.

Lunch trays in hand, Steve and Jase caught up with the gang and sat down.

"Hey, Jase. What's new?" Haley's voice teased.

"Haven't you heard? I can fly."

"Oh, I've heard. You're the only one at school who could get away with it too."

"But I …"

Jase thought about spilling his guts. And not the way he spilled them for Jeff. He wondered if his friends would understand dreams, his mother's phone call and having an Aunt Christy. Maybe the twins could help him understand what it means to go back so he could move forward.

"Can I sit here?" Brendan's voice quaked.

"MAY I sit here?" corrected Deirdre.

"Huh?"

"Never mind."

Danny and Deirdre slid over to make room. Brendan sat down. He breathed a great sigh of relief. Jill watched Brendan carefully eyeing the cafeteria.

"Hey, you don't need to worry," Jill assured him. "Jeff went home sick."

"What about his friends? They're still here."

"They aren't as tough when their leader is missing. Don't worry, eat your lunch."

Steve slid his lunch tray in front of Jase.

"Here, short-stuff, have some peaches on me. Sorry, they were fresh out of birdseed."

"Funny. Very funny."

It was funny though, and laughing at himself with a group of friends he trusted felt good. For a few moments he forgot about dreams, going back to move forward and his mom's mysterious phone call.

Chapter Thirty-Four:

Mrs. Ruppert stood at the door and smacked her lips.

We know … do not ask where Mr. Tims is today, it is not our business and she wouldn't tell us if she knew.

"Your instructions today are as follows: Mr. Tims has assigned groups of four to work together to complete a worksheet. Each group has a different worksheet. You are allowed to work together as long as you remember this is algebra, not the circus. Keep it down."

She called out the groups and the class assembled themselves accordingly. Jase was relieved to be grouped with Haley.

"Hey, Jase!" A voice called from across the room. "I bet you're gonna fly through this worksheet!"

Laughter boomed.

He tried to think of a clever come back, but Mrs. Ruppert unknowingly came to his rescue.

"Consider this your only warning. One more outburst by anyone in the class and the groups will receive a ten-point deduction on the worksheet."

Jase wished Mr. Tims was back from wherever or whatever. When he spoke of his faith Mr. Tims had a way of making him believe everything was going to be okay.

The last class of the day was replaced by a pep rally in honor of the first football game of the season. The entire school piled into the gym.

Principal Drew greeted the student body and said a lot of "I'm proud of this school," and "I know your conduct at this evening's game will show good sportsmanship," and of course, "There's nothing crummy about the Crumberry Middle School Wildcats!"

The football team made their entrance to screams and cheers from the stands and the sound of "We Will Rock You," blaring through the gymnasium speakers.

Principal Drew introduced Coach K who introduced each player by name, number, and position.

Coach K led the rally in reciting the pledge to the American flag.

The cheerleaders performed a cheer they had practiced since the summer. They instigated the crowd to do the wave while the drum corps pounded out a beat. The band played the school fight song.

As the pep rally came to a close, Principal Drew took the microphone one last time.

"Get those books and get your homework finished in time to show up and cheer on our team! Go! Fight! Win! Crumberry Middle School!"

The crowd roared with exuberant applause, full of pride for their school. The sound of heavy feet descending bleachers combined with excited chatter was almost deafening. The throng of kids got tighter the closer they got to the exits.

Someone shoved a folded-up piece of paper into Jase's hand. Whoever it was disappeared into the swarm of kids.

Jase waited until he was seated on the bus to unfold the paper.

WE WILL SETTLE THIS TONIGHT. MEET US BEHIND THE CONCESSION STAND ... UNLESS YOU'RE SCARED. THEN WE WILL COME FIND YOU.

Chapter Thirty-Five:

"I'll listen to the game on the radio and pick you up when it's over."

Jase waved as Aunt Christy drove away. It had been difficult to hide his relief when she told him she would rather not go to the game but would be glad to give him a ride.

Jase checked his back pocket to be sure his cell phone was safely tucked away. He knew his mom might try to call, just to check on him.

Groups of friends were gathered, all talking and laughing. The parents were already in the bleachers munching on nachos and popcorn.

Steve's dad quit snacking long enough to point out his son to the lady seated next to him.

"See him over there? Yeah, number thirty-two, that's my kid!"

"He looks like he eats you out of house and home!"

"Yup, yup. Gotta keep his energy up for these games. My boy's got talent. He's gonna go far. You got a kid on the team?"

"No, I'm here to watch my niece cheer. She's over there, the short redhead."

"Oh … good, good … we need our team spirit. Keep your eye on number 32. He's gonna go far."

The team finished the pregame warm up and jogged to the locker room for their final talk from Coach K.

The cheerleaders stretched a banner across the entrance to the field.

Jase stood by the fence that lined the field and waited for the team to break through the banner.

The percussion section of the band sounded a rata-tat-tat-tat and boom, boom, boom.

The boys pressed against each other and lurched forward like chained dogs. Coach K blew his whistle and the growling Crumberry Middle School Wildcats burst onto the field! The people in the home stands clapped and hooted and some even blew obnoxious air horns. No doubt the entire town was ready for the game!

The Wildcats and their opposing team stood at attention along their perspective sidelines. Each young man held his helmet in his left hand and placed his right hand over his heart. All eyes were riveted on the American flag as the national anthem played. Immediately following the song, a student led in the Our Father prayer.

Three players from each team marched to centerfield for the coin toss. The quarter flew into the air and descended in slow motion. The Wildcats won the toss and chose to receive the ball.

The shrill of a whistle and the game began.

Jase scanned both sets of bleachers in search of Jeff and his guys. He had not decided what he was going to do, and he had told no one.

"Hey, birdman, what's up?"

"ARGH! Haley, you scared me. Don't sneak up on a guy."

"Wow, why so jumpy?"

"I guess it's just been a long day. Listen, have you seen Jeff? Is he here?"

"Okay, go with that. Yeah, he's here. I saw him hanging out over by the concession stand."

Jase turned towards the concession stand and carefully surveyed the crowd. He couldn't find Jeff.

Is he still over there?

Maybe he is waiting behind the building … he expects me to meet him there.

Mom warned me not to fight with him.

I could go … we could talk …

Hey, Jeff, man, you don't want to beat me up, I'm just a pipsqueak
…

Um, hey, Jeff, sup, man?

Look, if you lay a finger on me I'm gonna throat punch you, so fight at your own risk!

Please, please, please don't hit me!

"What's the matter with you? You get weirder every day."

"Yeah, yeah I know. I guess it's not funny … is it?"

"No, it's just weird. What's going on?"

"Jeff wants me to meet him behind the concession stand. Said he wants to settle this with me … I guess this is because I didn't let him push Brendan around."

Jase continued to stare at the concessions stand as he waited for Haley to respond. Several uncomfortable seconds passed in silence. For the first time in the conversation, Jase looked at Haley.

Her eyes were wide with fear. Her normally pink cheeks were colorless. She was biting her bottom lip.

"Stop it, Haley. He's not gonna kill me. He'll probably just black my eyes or knock out my teeth … or paralyze me or something."

"That's not funny. Don't go. You'll end up in trouble. He's just a jerk, and it's not worth it."

"If I don't go this will never end. And besides, I don't want people sayin' I'm chicken."

"Why do boys have to be so stupid? Who cares if they call you chicken if you can keep your teeth?"

"Chicken have teeth?"

"Jase Freeman, you make me so mad!" And she turned and walked away. She didn't even look back over her shoulder at him. She just walked away.

Jase stuck his chin out and pulled his shoulders back. He took a deep breath and stepped towards the concessions stand.

On the way, he couldn't help but think *Here lies Jase Freeman...*

Chapter Thirty-Six:

Jase shoved his hands in his pockets as he neared the building. The sun had almost dipped below the horizon and the night air had turned chilly with no warning or was it fear that made him shiver?

He paused at the front of concessions. For a moment, he thought of buying a candy bar and skipping this crazy appointment.

Hello, God? It's me again. I wish my dad was here to tell me what to do. I want to do the right thing, but what is it? I'm going to face my fear. I'm going to face Jeff. I'm going to have faith that you will help me know what is right.

He stepped to the back of the building to see if there was any sign Jeff had been there. A grove of trees surrounded the backside of the building with a little over ten feet of clearance. Enough room for several trash cans that smelled of stale nachos and chili dogs. The shadows of the night made it a creepy place to be. He swallowed hard and turned in a tight circle, carefully looking for Jeff's posse.

No one was there.

What a break!

I showed up, Jeff, where were you?

Did ya chicken out? It's a good thing, you mighta lost your teeth!

He breathed a sigh of relief and turned to leave.

SNAP!

The sound of a heavy foot placing its weight on a fallen branch thundered through Jase's chest.

He wanted to run. Using every ounce of self-control, Jase turned to find himself the center of attention. Jeff and his boys stood before him, the crowded stands of cheering fans were behind him. No one stood next to him.

"Well, lookie here, boys. The midget actually showed up. Had any more pancakes today, Jase?"

"Do you really need the boys with you, Jeff? I'm not gonna puke on you again. You can probably handle this on your own."

"The boys are here to watch and learn."

Jase stared back at Jeff, looking him in the eyes without blinking. Jeff was visibly uncomfortable, but it was clear he wasn't backing down.

He determined at that moment he was not going to fight with anyone. Jeff could hit him but he was not going to hit back. Even as he made this decision, fear crept slowly up his spine like a snake weaving back and forth. A shudder moved through him, and Jeff laughed.

Jeff stepped forward and grabbed Jase's shirt. He leaned in, placing his face so close to Jase's face their noses almost touched. Jeff's foul, hot breath settled around Jase's neck.

Jase wanted to cry but knew what had to be done.

"Go ahead. Do it now, Jeff. Hit me."

Jeff squinted, whispered through his teeth, "What are you doing?"

"I'm not doing anything; it's all on you. You want to hit me? Well, hit me then."

The cheering from the crowd in the stands roared like thunder.

"Are you scared?"

"Why don't you just hit me?"

"Look, kid, I do what I want, when I want. Don't tell me when to hit you."

Jeff let go of Jase's shirt and gave him a shove, causing him to stumble backwards and fall to the ground. He could smell the nasty nachos he landed in but didn't dare move. He made the snap decision to stay on the ground, thinking it would make it difficult for Jeff to knock his teeth out.

"Get up."

Jase looked up at the giant Jeff and didn't say a word.

"I said get up."

"TOUCHDOWN Wildcats!" rang over the PA system and the crowd went crazy.

"I get it," muttered Jase.

"You what?"

"I said I get it. I understand. I know what it's like."

"Are you crazy?"

"No. Yes. Maybe."

"And stupid. You're pretty stupid."

"Yeah, maybe. But I know what it's like ... to be ... well, for your mom to have to work so hard." Jase swallowed hard.

He hadn't planned to say it, but now it was done. He took a chance after what Mrs. Zimmers had said ... Some kids turn into bullies because picking on others somehow is a distraction to the hurt inside.

Jeff's eyes blazed as he glared down at Jase. His jaw clenched tightly as he moved his gaze from Jase to the crowded stands behind him and back to Jase. Without another word, Jeff walked away.

The posse looked on in disbelief before following their leader.

As soon as he was alone with the scent of stale nachos and chili dogs, Jase laid back into the cool grass and gazed up at the starry sky. His cheeks glistened with nervous perspiration, and his heart had not yet received the message that the danger was past. He took a deep breath. He thought of nights gone by when he and his mom stargazed together. He thought of the mysterious phone call he'd overheard, and he wondered what it would be like to wish on a star and no longer worry about people he loved.

He wondered what it would be like to one day be friends with the biggest bully at Crumberry Middle School.

Chapter Thirty-Seven:

The "ping" of a text coming through interrupted Jase's wondering. He sat up and dug his phone out of his back pocket.

Hey, son, how's the game going? You okay?

Jase walked back to the fence line and checked the scoreboard, up by seven with three minutes left to the first half.

It's all good. We are up by seven,

That's great! Have fun and stay out of trouble, k?

Yes, ma'am.

He wondered if his mom would be proud of how he handled Jeff or disappointed that he went to meet him.

Halftime began and the band marched to the center of the field. The announcer introduced them with great excitement, "Hey, fans, stand to your feet and welcome the award-winning Crumberry Middle School marching band! Tonight's performance is brought to you by the '70s in a throwback presentation of 'Fly Like an Eagle' first recorded by the Steve Miller Band in 1976."

The crowd thundered their applause. The wind instruments began with a "dooooo, dooooo, doo, doo" and the flag corps marched to the beat.

Are you kidding me? Fly like an eagle?

Jase wasn't sure if he should laugh, cry, or throw up.

Danny and Deirdre walked up and stood next to Jase.

"Hey," greeted Deirdre.

"Oh, hey, guys! How great is this? We are winning our first game."

"Did you see that great play Steve made? His dad went nuts, hollering 'That's my boy! That's my boy! He's gonna go far I tell ya!' I wonder if Steve could hear him out on the field." Danny shook his head in amazement.

"Uh … no, I missed that play. I … uh … was busy."

Haley bounced up wearing a huge grin.

"I want to fly like an eagle, to be free … fly like an eagle," she sang along as the band played.

The twins laughed in harmony.

"Ha. Ha. Ha," Jase pretended to be annoyed. He didn't want his friends to know how embarrassed he continued to be.

"Oh, come on, Jase, you have to admit it couldn't be funnier. It's like they planned it. Or you planned it."

"I promise you, I had nothing to do with it."

The band wrapped up the performance. Jase could not have been readier for the game to get under way. The team rushed the field and the second half began. Danny, Deirdre, and Haley stood with Jase along the fence under the goal post.

In a matter of a few plays, the Wildcats had scored two more touchdowns.

"I wonder what Coach K told them in the locker room. They were playing great in the first half but now, they are awesome!" Haley was so excited she couldn't stand still.

"There's no tellin'. Maybe he threatened to make 'em all run tomorrow if they didn't hit the field all in."

"All in? All in what?" Danny could easily explain the theory of relativity, but his mind didn't grasp simple sayings.

"All in the game, as in giving it all they got."

"Have to give. Don't you mean have to give, Jase?" Deirdre's eyebrows were both raised. She looked a lot like Mrs. Zimmers.

"Help me out, Jill."

134

"Mmmmm, nope. I'll sit this one out."

"Never mind, guys. Whatever coach said, the team listened."

"Let's go get some nachos." Once again, the twins spoke in perfect unison.

How do they do that?

"Speaking of nachos," said Haley as she reached for Jase's collar, pulling a half-eaten nacho chip from his jacket. "This is disgusting."

"Haven't you heard? This is Calvin Klein's latest scent. It's called 'Nacho Night.' I almost lost my teeth for it."

Haley wasn't amused. Even as he pretended, Jase wasn't either.

Chapter Thirty-Eight:

He was glad his mom was in bed and Aunt Christy was not in her normal chatty, nosy mood. She had tried to mess his hair up when they got home. Her hand touched the cheese before she got to his hair.

"Jase, son, last time I checked nachos go in your mouth, not behind your ears."

"Good night, Aunt Christy. Thanks for the ride."

The hot shower felt good. The gooey cheese that had begun to crust over had left him thinking he would never eat nachos again.

Jase's mind replayed what happened with Jeff as the heat melted away the stench of stale food. He still wasn't convinced he had done the right thing, but he wasn't sure it was wrong either.

Dad would have known what to do.

Jase shut his bedroom door and walked over to the window. It was almost ten o'clock. The night sky's shining lights were cloaked in clouds.

Lecty hopped up on Jase's shoulder without a sound. It was as if she knew his heart was heavy. She puffed her feathers and settled in close to his neck. He looked up at the gloom of night and quietly spoke to Lecty.

"See all those clouds up there? They block our view of the stars, but the stars are still there. The stars are always there. Lecty, if we hang in there long enough, the clouds will float away and the stars will shine through."

Lecty whispered back, "Rawk, hang in therrrrrrre. Hang in there."

Jase stood at the window for a long time. Lecty nuzzled next to his neck.

And behind those clouds, there's a star that will light the way for Mom if I wish hard enough.

He helped Lecty back to her perch and edged into bed.

His mind replayed his long day. He wished he could quiet the voices in his head. From his mom's phone call last night, to his debut as a bird in science class, to Mrs. Zimmers' teary-eyed talk. Hurting people hurt people. That talk had given him the courage to face Jeff at the game. It had been quite a day. He couldn't forget the moment he lost his pancakes all over Jeff's T-shirt and gym shoes.

He tossed and turned, trying in vain to get comfortable. Sometime after midnight, he finally fell asleep.

Jase opened his eyes, but he dared not move. The vibrant blue sky above him held no clouds. It was beautiful. An energetic green glowed at the corners of his eyes. He turned his head enough to see strands of sweet smelling grass. The greenest green grass he had ever seen. As he sat up, he felt every muscle in his body twinge and ache. Had someone beat him or had a tree fallen on him?

A flutter of color swooped over his head, doing a few loops in the sky before floating to the ground in front of him.

It was the giant, bulgy-eyed butterfly. Jase held his breath and waited for the WAH-FOOF of multi-colored, nasty tasting cloud of yuck.

The bug's mouth opened. Jase leaned away.

"You cannot fly."

"What?"

"You cannot fly. Such a disappointment, too. I thought you would soar."

"Yeah, well I am sore alright."

"That's because you cannot fly, but you can fall."

"I fell?" Jase panicked. He checked himself for broken bones.

The butterfly laughed. A small amount of the unforgiving mist escaped the corners of his mouth.

"I helped you with your landing. After all, we've traveled a long way back together."

"What? I've made it back? Where's back?"

"Look around you, boy. You are back."

"What do I do now?"

"Not to worry Jase, you'll figure it out."

The butterfly began its swirl upward.

"Don't leave me. You have to help me! How will I figure it out?"

"You'll know when the time is right."

"Wait! How will I know? I don't know! Don't go, please help me! How will I know?"

The bug began to break apart, like a detailed mosaic with the spaces between the colored pieces growing wider by the millisecond. Just before the colors fully dissipated, the air around him whispered, "You'll know when the time is right."

Jase remained seated as he turned his head to the right and carefully began to survey his surroundings.

There were trees.

Squirrels.

Birds singing.

And a field covered in wild flowers.

He continued to look and listen as he turned to his left.

There was a tractor tire sandbox.

An old swing.

Monkey bars.

A ball.

And, in the distance, the large, bulgy-eyed butterfly, perched on a tall blade of grass.

Chapter Thirty-Nine:

She quietly opened her son's bedroom door and stole across the room. She stood for a few minutes watching him sleep. The moon and stars cast shadows through the window. The shadows danced over his face.

Her thoughts took her many places.

He's such a good kid. Even when he messes up, he learns from his mistakes. I'm so proud of this kid and thankful he's mine.

He looks more like his daddy as he grows. The picture Justin's mom gave me of Justin when he was Jase's age ... they could be the same person. Oh, Justin, you would be so proud too.

She thought of how good it was to have Christy here to watch over him this weekend while she was away.

Maybe he won't ask about me in the morning.

Maybe he won't know I'm gone until he gets home from school in the afternoon.

She lovingly brushed his hair to one side and kissed his forehead.

I love you, Jasey.

◎ ◎ ◎

The sun rose and called for Jase to get dressed for the last day of school before the weekend.

He moved slowly as he dressed. Not because he had plenty of time but more because he was sore from getting shoved to the ground last night. Bruised as he might have been, he was grateful he still had his teeth.

Maybe Jeff beat me up after all ...

Relieved to see cereal and a bowl on the kitchen table, he had already decided not to eat a big breakfast. Yesterday's pancakes were too fresh in his memory.

"Morning."

"Good morning, Jase. Did you get any sleep?"

"Enough. Where's Mom?"

"I haven't seen her yet this morning. Must still be in bed. Leave the clothes you wore to the game last night where I can find them, please. I'm gonna get the cheese washed out before it sets in."

"Okay, thanks."

Aunt Christy mumbled something about wishing she knew how he managed to get nacho cheese sauce in his hair and on his clothes. Jase was glad she didn't ask.

Spoons clinked against the bowls as he and Aunt Christy ate without conversation. Aside from the occasional bark of a neighborhood dog, it was a quiet way to begin the day. No shrill laughter, no hair mess-ups, no pokes in the gut.

Stealing a glance her way, Jase wondered if Aunt Christy was sick or something. After checking the time, he decided not to ask.

He put his bowl in the sink and went back to his room to grab his backpack. He gathered last night's cheesy clothes and piled them on the floor by his bed.

He tossed Lecty a piece of dried fruit, "Have a good day, girl. Behave while I'm at school."

"Rawk! Tiiiime! Riiiiight tiiimmme!"

"What did you say?"

"RAWK!"

"Wow, I'm hearing things."

Aunt Christy waited at the front door.

"Tell Mom I hope she has a good day."

"I will … but what about me? What am I? Chopped liver?"

"What? Chopped liver?"

"Oh, forget it. I guess you're too young to have heard that one."

"Yeah, well … hope you have a good day too. Thanks for washing my clothes."

"Glad to do it, kid!" She poked him in the stomach and laughed.

Jase wondered if Aunt Christy would be going home soon. He had heard it said house guests and fish have something in common: they both stink after three days. Guilt washed over him as he thought of how much help she had been to his mom this week.

He gave her a quick hug, "See ya this afternoon."

Aunt Christy rocked back on her heals in utter disbelief that Jase had hugged her.

Jase couldn't believe it himself. Maybe he loved her after all.

The jog to the bus ushered the voices back in his head.

What did Mom's phone call mean?

How will I know what to do when the time is right?

How will I know when the time is right?

Will Jeff be waiting for me?

Chapter Fourty:

Friday is every school kid's favorite day of the week. Jase wondered if he had ever wanted a day to pass quickly more than he wanted this day to be over.

Homeroom was celebratory as Principal Drew congratulated the football team on their win.

"I'm proud of my school! You boys played the game with class and came out on top. Our band performed to award winning standards and the cheerleaders ... well ... they didn't drop anybody! Great job, CMS! Now, don't go getting full of yourselves. There's another game next week; pride always comes before a fall. Have a great Friday and stay safe this weekend!"

As the kids crammed into the hall for first period, Mr. Houston put his hand on Jase's shoulder.

"This is your last weekend before the Bully Free Zone Conference. Are you ready?"

"Yes, sir, I have some ideas that might just work. Do you want me to go over them with you?"

"I think that's a good idea, but I have to leave for the day at 10:00. Mr. Tims is part of the Bully Free Zone committee. See if he has a few minutes to meet with you."

"Is he back today? He's been out the last two days."

"He's here. See if he has time."

"Yes, sir. I sure will!"

Jase could not have been happier to hear Mr. Tims was back. So glad, in fact, he felt like he was walking on air. He was excited to tell Mr. Tims about his ideas for the conference. He was relieved to know Mrs. Ruppert would not be there. He wasn't sure which was worse—the way she sucked her teeth or her lack of a sense of humor.

The day was already way better than he thought it could possibly be.

As Jase neared the science room, he heard Mr. Tims' laughter. He turned to see him rolling down the hall, talking with Coach K about the game. Coach slapped him on the back and turned down the hall that led to the gym.

"Sweet!" Jase hustled over to Mr. Tims. "Hey! You're back!"

"Yup, how's it going Jase? Anything gone wrong lately?"

"Oh, you have no idea. We don't have time right now to get into it. I have a question though."

"I might have an answer."

"Mr. Houston said it would be good for me to go over my ideas for the Bully Free Zone Conference before next week, but he can't help me today. He said to ask you if you have time."

"Well, my day is pretty packed after being out. I tell you what, if you can stay after school, I can give you a ride home."

"Awesome! I'll try to call Mom and see if it's okay."

"How about you go on to class. I'll call your mom."

"Thanks, Mr. Tims! See ya later!"

Yes, this day was definitely better than he thought it would be.

Chapter Fourty-One:

Jase scrambled into gym class, relieved to get in before the bell. Coach K had his own answer to tardy kids. Any kid caught coming in after the bell knew to drop and give Coach fifty while the rest of the class counted.

"In honor of our first win of the season, I will go easy on you today. The sun is shining, and we all need some extra vitamin D before winter hits. Everybody out! We are walking the track today. Let's get our ten thousand steps in!"

No one grumbled. Walking the track was much better than sprinting the track. Groups of friends huddled up. The chatter began as they walked.

"Did you see Steve's big play last night?"

"The band was awesome!"

"I heard there was a fight behind the concession stand."

None of the bus-stop gang were in Jase's PE class. His mom always said, "If you want to have friends, you have to be friendly." Jase took that to heart and had made friends with anyone willing.

He stayed quiet as kids yammered on about the game last night and plans for the weekend. His thoughts were rambling again.

Butterflies. His mom's phone call. Aunt Christy. Almost there. Knowing when the time is right.

Jase tripped on his own shoelace, nearly planted his face on the unforgiving track surface. He stopped long enough to double knot the rebellious shoestring.

As he began to stand up, part of Jeff's cohort came from behind and stood over him.

Great. Now what? I knew this day was going too good.

There they stood, three not-so-big guys, glaring at him.

Should I sit down or stand up?

"Are you brave or stupid?"

"Maybe we should take care of him now."

"Yeah, he kinda has it comin' from all of us."

Jase braced himself for the coming face punch. He closed both eyes and held his breath.

But nothing happened.

He cautiously peered out of one eye.

There on the ground in front of him was the giant shadow of someone standing behind him.

Steve to the rescue!

The dread covered him like a blanket when he turned and saw the owner of the shadow wasn't Steve at all.

Jeff towered above him.

Jeff's boys stood in front of him.

Not a friend in sight.

"Leave the runt alone."

"But Jeff ..."

"I said leave him be."

Time stood still as Jeff's henchmen stood dumbfounded.

Jeff reached his hand down to Jase and pulled him to his feet.

No words were spoken between them. The bully's eyes were intent on Jase. Jase's knees weakened, as if they were made of cooked spaghetti. He set his gaze on Jeff.

He searched for a sign of what was to come.

Was he about to be pounded?

Would Jeff verbally assault him before pounding him?

Are there any words in the English language that could prevent this beating?

Suspended in the timeless twilight zone, the tension in the air grew heavier by the millisecond.

Jeff's eyes, the eyes that had glared at Jase last night, were no longer angry. The enormous bully of CMS, ruler of hallways, fear-caster, stood in front of Jase and looked him square in the eyes. Without a word, he gave an ever so slight, crooked smile.

And walked away.

Chapter Fourty-Two:

The rest of gym class was a blur as Jase tried to decide if Jeff had given him a momentary reprieve or if he had witnessed something new in Jeff's eyes? There was a kind of softness. Almost the look of friendship.

The bell rang and Jase shoved his books in his locker. No homework this weekend! YEAH!

Jase ambled into Mr. Tims' classroom just as the last student left.

"Pull up a chair." Mr. Tims sat behind his desk.

"Thanks for staying after school for me."

"No problem. I'm anxious to hear your ideas."

"Well, I thought about it a lot. I think my best idea is 'Choose or Lose, Bully Free Me.'"

Jase went on to explain the variations. Choose Friendship. Choose Kindness. Choose Forgiveness.

"The thing is, being bully free is up to each one of us. It's all about choices."

"I think these ideas are great! They are even better when put into practice. Have you had a chance to do that, Jase?"

Jase wondered if Mr. Tims had heard the rumors that floated around the school halls. He wondered if Mr. Houston had told him about the tripping incident. He wondered if he knew what Mrs. Zimmers had told him.

"Yes, sir, I've learned a lot this week. I know it feels terrible to choose revenge. I don't want to be a bully. Not even to the bully."

"What choices have you made this week?"

"I chose revenge first. Then I chose to try to understand. Does that make sense?"

"I don't know the whole story, but yes, it does. I think this 'Choose or Lose' slogan has a lot of possibilities."

"Thanks!"

"You ready to head home?"

"Yes, sir, whenever you are. Hey, can I ask you a question?"

"Sure."

"How do you drive? I mean, the wheelchair and all."

"My truck is a souped-up quad cab with a lift to get my chair behind the wheel. I have special hand controls so I can drive without needing my legs."

"That's pretty cool!"

"Technology is great when it works for ya!"

"Can I ask another question? It's pretty personal."

"Go ahead and ask. I'll decide if it's too personal."

"Mrs. Ruppert didn't tell the class where you were. I worried that you got sick or something. Were you sick? Where were you?"

Mr. Tims looked out the classroom window. He watched the football players warming up for practice as if he was buying time to find the right words.

"I'm sorry. I shouldn't have asked."

"No, no it's okay. I'll tell you where I was. When the leaves on the trees change color and begin to coat the ground, I make the drive over to a special cemetery."

"Cemetery?" Jase was sorry he had asked such a personal question. He wished he could have a redo. He would have skipped this question.

"I go back and spend time among the brave men and women who gave their lives for the freedoms we enjoy in America. I go back and place a remembrance at the graves of my brothers who sacrificed everything. I make peace with the fact that I am here, and they are not. I make a recommitment to make the most of my days here on earth, to never take a single breath for granted."

Jase understood. He was young when his dad didn't come home. He kept his picture on his desk in his room. Sometimes he felt proud. Sometimes he felt sad. But he always felt awe. His dad was his hero.

Jase looked at Mr. Tims as Mr. Tims looked out the window. For the first time since the school year began, he realized Mr. Tims was his hero too.

The silence was long but surprisingly, not at all uncomfortable. Mr. Tims' mind had traveled back to his recent visit. Jase respected the pause.

"Well," Mr. Tims turned to Jase. "Let's get you home."

"Oh, hey, I guess my mom said it was okay for you to bring me home then?"

"Not exactly, I didn't talk to your mom. I spoke with someone named Christy. She said it was okay."

"Aunt Christy? Where was my mom?"

"She said your mom had left town and wouldn't be back until Sunday."

A sickening lump rose to Jase's throat and threatened to choke him. His eyes burned as he blinked back the tears caused by the unknown. He didn't want to cry in front of Mr. Tims. He didn't want to cry at all.

"You okay, Jase?"

"Yes, I mean, no. Not really. No."

"What's going on? Any way I can help?"

"Well, my mom ... she's been ... well she's just ... no, sir, I don't think so."

"Let's get you home. Your Aunt Christy will have answers for you."

The truck windows were down and refreshing fall air blew in, trying to bring energy to Jase. He glanced at the colors in the trees, the reds, oranges, and yellows that his mom said God caused when he dipped the end of his brush in the paints and flicked the colors over the horizon.

He wondered if he would ever see the sparkle in his mother's eyes again.

Chapter Fourty-Three:

Christy came running out of the house, wildly waving a piece of paper.

"Jase, I'm sorry. I didn't know. I wouldn't have let her go alone. I didn't know! I thought she was sleeping in. She's been so tired. When it was almost lunch time, and I hadn't heard from her, I checked in on her. She was gone, and I found this on her pillow."

Dear Christy and Jase,

I'm sorry I didn't let you know what is going on. I knew you would worry and try to stop me. Mom's letter made me realize I need to make peace with my past. I am going home to see Mom. Chris, take care of Jase. I will be back Sunday.

I love both of you,

Jancey aka Mom

Worry lines etched themselves across his face.

"Aunt Christy, will you take me to Mom?"

"Oh, Jase. I don't know. I'm a nervous wreck. I just don't know."

"How far is it? I can take you. I can take both of you." Mr. Tims looked at Christy and then at Jase. "I don't mind."

"We can't ask you to do that, Mr. Tims."

"Well, now, you didn't ask. I offered."

Jase and Aunt Christy looked at each other for a moment. Jase nodded yes.

"Let me lock up the house," Christy turned and went back inside.

"I'll be right back. I need something from my room."

Jase sprinted to his desk and gingerly picked up the envelope that sheltered the discolored treasure map from his mother's childhood.

Jase couldn't remember how long it took to get to Grandma Lynny's. He had been just a little boy the last time they had visited her. He remembered her apple trees and the free-range chickens. He always thought her house looked like it had a face—windows for eyes and the door for its mouth. He remembered pictures on the fireplace mantel of the granddad he never knew. He wondered if the fat orange cat would still be there.

Jase was grateful for Mr. Tims' offer to drive them. He didn't have confidence in Aunt Christy's ability to get them there safely.

He sat in the back seat, staring anxiously out the window. He wished he could see stars in the daylight. Maybe he would make a wish.

Instead, he prayed.

God, I don't understand what is happening. I'm scared. I'm worried about my mom. She needs your strength. She needs faith that gives her joy.

He listened as Mr. Tims and Aunt Christy talked about the weather, country music, and homemade biscuits.

He rested his head against the window and drifted off to sleep.

Chapter Fourty-Four:

Jase stood near the tractor tire sandbox. Weeds poked through the surface in uneven rebellion. A cracked, faded-yellow pail lay partially buried in the once free-flowing sand. It had obviously been many years since small hands built castles here.

The swing hung a few yards away. Statuesque, but the days of glee-filled squeals of joy were long gone.

This place was so different from any other he had ever visited. Tiny feet made to explore were missing from this yard, yet it was vibrant and full of life. Jase thought of all the hill climbing, red dirt and rocky terrain he had recently experienced. The scene before him now was the polar opposite.

Two tiny, multi-colored butterflies twirled by, one chasing the other in a corkscrew of flight. He watched them as twisted their way to the house. Each landed on a perfect red rose that grew on a bush near Grandma Lynny's back door.

Chickadees sang in the pine trees as squirrels raced past them.

The brilliantly blue sky almost paled in comparison to the emerald green grass. A slight breeze blew past him.

Jase turned a slow circle, capturing every sight for his remember-this-forever file. The apple orchard ripe with fall delight, Grandma Lynny's clothesline with sheets swaying in the breeze, and the small white farmhouse on the hill with windows and a door that looked like a face, all locked in perfect preservation in his mind. And in his heart.

A soft, multicolored wing brushed against his ear as the bulgy-eyed butterfly rested on his shoulder.

"Well done, Jase. You no longer need me."

"Where are you going? Will I see you again?"

"I have no answers. Just two words. You're smiling," it whispered in a voice as smooth as Grandma Lynny's homemade applesauce.

"I am, aren't I?"

"You've made it, Jase. Can you feel it?"

"Yes, I feel it. I didn't know ..."

"Yes?"

"How sad and worried my insides were until the sad and worry went away. Now that they are gone, well ... I can't stop smiling."

"Your journey is almost complete, Jase. You have one more thing you must do. Someone else is still sad and worried."

The butterfly gently lifted off his shoulder and silently hovered in the air. Jase set his gaze beyond the swing to the row of trees in the distance.

"It's time, my young friend, it's time." The butterfly glided on the breeze like a kite in weightless wonder as it floated to the trees and rested ...

On a tall blade of grass.

Chapter Fourty-Five:

"It's time to wake up Jase, we will be at Grandma Lynny's in a few minutes."

Aunt Christy reached to the back seat and patted Jase on the knee. He rubbed his eyes.

I wonder how long I slept.

Rounding a bend in the road, Jase looked up and saw Grandma Lynny's white house. Just as he remembered it, the house with a face was looking back.

The truck rolled to a stop next to his mother's car. Without a second thought, Jase was out of the truck.

"Mom? Mom!" He called out as he raced to the side of the house.

She stood next to the swing, both of her hands holding on as if she might take a seat and ask someone to give her a push. She let go of the swing and gave Jase a hug.

"Mom, are you okay? We were … we are worried. Are you okay?"

"I will be. As soon as I find it …" She looked away, searching the corners of the yard.

Jase pulled the envelope from his back pocket. "Let's find it together."

She gasped. Both hands on her mouth and her eyes wide.

"Where did you …?"

"Aunt Christy gave it to me."

She gingerly unfolded the paper, handling it as if it were a fragile piece of glass. She silently studied the map. She took Jase by the hand, straightened up tall, and together they walked to the edge of the row of trees.

They found a patch of ground surrounded by tall grass.

"Wait," said Jase as he ran back to the sandbox and dug near the pail. He pulled a once red plastic shovel from its hiding place and dusted it off as he sprinted back to his mom.

Her hand shook as she scooped loose soil to the side.

"Curious," she remarked, "it shouldn't be this easy to dig here after all these years."

A thud rang in the air like the sound of a baseball knocked out of the park.

Chapter Fourty-Six:

Her tired eyes were moist as she dusted off the top of a box. She lifted it out of its hiding place and sat it on the ground between them.

"Open it, Jase."

This is it. We are here and this is it.

Jase licked his lips out of nervous anticipation and nudged the lid of the box to the side.

They gazed inside at a small blue book with the inscription "Diary" on the front. She held the book, cradled it next to her heart for a moment then calmly opened it to the last page that contained writing.

She read aloud,

Dear Diary,

I miss my dad. And if I could talk to him, I would tell him thank you for being my dad. I would tell him I miss him. I would tell him one day I will marry someone just like him. My dad. My hero.

"I've thought about this diary often over the years. I just couldn't remember where I had buried it and I lost the map. I used to sit out here under these trees and write and imagine what it would be like to have my dad back."

They sat in silence together for several minutes. Their hearts connected by life without a dad. They understood each other.

"What's this?" Jase picked up an envelope with his name on it.

"I ... I don't know. That's strange. I was a child when I buried this box. I didn't put this here."

Jase's hands were the ones that quivered as he broke the seal and pulled the letter from the envelope.

He read to his mom,

I gave this letter to your Grandma Lynny before I left with instructions to give it to you if I didn't make it home. I had no doubt she would know when the time was right.

You and your momma are God's best gift to me. I didn't leave this earth by choice, but I hope you will one day understand that I would do it all again.

There comes a time when a man must stand for what is right, stand in the gap for those who cannot stand for themselves. You will learn soon enough there are all kinds of people in this world. When you find yourself looking the bad guy in the eyes, don't be afraid to stand.

Take good care of your mom, and never doubt my love.

Dad

Jase swallowed hard as emotion gripped his throat. A ray of sun caused a bright glint to shine from inside the box.

He held his breath as he lifted a frame from the box containing a bronze star attached to a red ribbon with the letter "V" on it.

"Mom?"

"I am confused too, Jase, I don't know how that got in the box. I gave this to Grandma Lynny to put in safekeeping." She glanced towards the house and she pushed her hair behind her ears.

"Son, this is a Bronze Star with Valor. It is awarded to military personnel in honor of combat heroism. Your dad gave his life saving the life of one of his brothers-in-arms. Your dad is a he … hero … I married a hero."

"My dad will always be my hero."

Jase hugged his mom.

She kissed the top of her son's head.

"Momma, it's a star. A star to light your way."

"It is a very special star."

"Can we take it home? We need to put it where you will see it every day. It will help you to remember you married your hero. It's the only star you need."

"Yes, Jase. We will take it home with us. I want to display it in a special place." Her voice was strong and her smile was sure. "But you know what? I need to take a look at the blanket of stars in the nighttime sky. Maybe tonight, we'll grab that purple afghan and do some star gazing?"

Jase saw the sparkle in his mom's eyes and his heart felt the joy he had so deeply missed.

"Yeah! Let's do it!"

They stood and hugged. For the first time in many years Jase knew everything would be okay.

Was it his dreams and the guiding of that bulging-eyed butterfly?

Was it the star he'd wished on?

Was it the Bronze Star?

Was it the God Mr. Tims had faith in and taught him to believe in too?

One thing was certain. Jase was no longer dreaming.

Mom stepped back and held Jase's face in her hands.

"I love you, Jasey. You make me one proud Momma!"

"Thanks, Ma. I love you too!"

Jase picked up the box, handling it with care.

"Was the ride up here tons of fun with your Aunt Christy?"

"Aunt Christy didn't … oh no! I left Mr. Tims in the truck with her!"

"Mr. Tims?"

"Yeah, he drove. They talked. I slept." Jase grinned.

"We better rescue him." She winked. "Hey, do you think Grandma Lynny has any apple pie? Race ya!"

Jase watched his mom laughing as she hurried towards the house.

Mr. Tims and Aunt Christy looked on from the driveway.

Grandma Lynny gazed at the scene through the kitchen window. She wiped the tears from her cheeks with her dish towel and smiled with satisfaction as she put her small gardening shovel back on the hook in the pantry.

High above the house, a giant bulgy eyed multi-colored butterfly smiled and fluttered away.

Mr. Tims watched as Jase lifted the framed Bronze Star out of the box. He smiled through the tears that stained his face. *I will keep my promise to you, Justin Freeman, I owe you my life.*

About The Author

Shelley Pierce grew up in rural Minnesota. The memories of the outdoor wonderland of childhood continue to influence her writing.

Shelley and her husband, Tommy, live in the foothills of the Smokey Mountains of East Tennessee. Here they raised their four children and now enjoy the gift of grandchildren. Tommy is the senior pastor of Towering Oaks Baptist Church, and Shelley serves alongside him on staff as the director of preschool and children's ministries.

Shelley understands the challenges today's children face. She enjoys the friendships, laughter, and even the struggles of ministering in the lives of kids. Every experience presents an opportunity to learn more about God's great love.

Writing experience includes various curriculums for "LifeWay Childhood Publications" (known as "LifeWay Kids"), "The Upper Room," "Power for Living," and as a contributor to "The Mighty Pen, Short and Sweet," and "Guideposts: The Joys of Christmas 2016."

CPSIA information can be obtained
at www.ICGtesting.com
Printed in the USA
LVOW10s0618201117
556986LV00026B/740/P

9 781946 638496